THE GATE

THE GATE

ISABELLA

SAPPHIRE BOOKS

SALINAS, CALIFORNIA

Book Design - LJ Reynolds
Cover Design - Treehouse Studio
Editor - Shelley Thrasher

Sapphire Books Publishing, LLC
P.O. Box 8142
Salinas, CA 93912
www.sapphirebooks.com

Printed in the United States of America
Second Edition – October 2017

This and other Sapphire Books titles can be found at
www.sapphirebooks.com

Other Books by Isabella

American Yakuza Series
American Yakuza I
The Lies that Bind – American Yakuza II
Razor's Edge – American Yakuza III

Forever Faithful Series
Always Faithful
Forever Faithful

Executive Series
Executive Disclosure
Surviving Reagan

Scarlet Series
Scarlet Masquerade
Scarlet Assassin

Broken Series
Broken Shield

Erotic shorts
Last Train

Dedication

For my mom.

May she be in Valhalla raising hell.

Schileen

I am for ever your paladin.

Acknowledgments

Thanks to the village, Heather Flournoy, Shelley Thrasher, Connie Ward, and others who made this book possible.

Prologue

Jerking off her leather armor chest guard, Dawn let it fall to the floor in a fit of rage. She kicked the leather across the floor, pissed that she had to train in secret. Her new duties for her charge wouldn't begin until the afternoon, when Aphrodite finally woke for the day. She ran her fingers over the birthmark on her chest, a constant reminder that she had larger duties ahead of her.

"Mother!" Dawn screamed. "How could you do this to me? Of all the goddesses, you had to pick Aphrodite?"

"Daughter."

Dawn cringed. She hadn't really expected a response.

"She will teach you the most valuable lesson of all," said her mother. Omniscient that she was, her mother granted very few the pleasure of her presence. Why was Dawn surprised she wasn't one of them? "You will learn patience being Aphrodite's handmaiden, my daughter. You'll need it for your Paladin. She has yet to perfect that virtue and will need the guidance of someone like you."

"But, but...Allie got to serve the goddess of war. Why couldn't I learn from the huntress, or somebody equally spectacular?"

"Your sister is learning to fight her own battles. She has yet to prove that she can handle a Paladin. You, my dear, will be the protector of The Chosen One, and she will stress you to your limit. Trust me, you'll thank me for this little exercise. Now go back to Aphrodite and fulfill your job. Besides, your time is almost done here."

"I can't believe this."

Dawn's mother's voice, tinny in her ear, reminded her of the great challenge that was to come. Powerful forces wanted Earth to spin off its axis, causing it to go dark. Lately, the Paladins were failing in their struggle to bring lost souls to their next gate, so it was imperative that the Protectors be ready for a higher battle.

"Dawn! Where are you, sweetie?" Aphrodite's singsong voice rang through the great halls.

"Shit." Dawn tucked her wings and pulled her gown on, tying the belt loosely. "Coming."

"There you are." Aphrodite hugged Dawn and laced her fingers through Dawn's. "I need a bath and require someone to scrub my back." Pulling Dawn along, Aphrodite turned and smiled. "Would you be a dear and bring something to eat…oh, and some wine, too. I'm famished."

Dawn closed her eyes, her jaw bunched as she cursed under her breath. "Of course."

Chapter One

Harley's head hurt. Her mind felt like it was on fucking overload. All she'd done was think all day. That's all she could do now. The hike had been a chance to reevaluate her life, assess where she wanted to be and where she was going. Instead, it had become more than self-reflection; it had undone her. No phone, no computer, no TV—completely off the grid. Technology had replaced everyone's ability to really communicate, so she'd left it all behind—tossed her cell phone out of the car's window as she'd sped down the highway and watched in her driver's side mirror as it busted into tiny little pieces, never to be reclaimed, not even if she wanted to. She didn't.

Being alone off the grid let her think, made her think of what had happened.

No TV, no diversions. People vegetated for years in a state of misery because of TV, didn't they? TV allowed them to focus on something other than their own miserable lives, their pain, and their inadequacies. Hell, watch it long enough, and if you weren't depressed and miserable, you soon were.

Looking down, she ran her hand over her stomach, feeling her pelvic bones. Dinnertime. She'd lost her appetite long ago. *Maybe I'll get nutritional dementia.* When had she last had something solid in her stomach? The pain had replaced hunger a long time ago. *Thank God.* Staring at the protein bar she was holding, she couldn't imagine downing another tasteless piece of cardboard. She tossed it into the fire. She didn't want wild animals digging through her campsite while she was there asleep.

Arrroooo. A coyote howled off in the distance, signaling the impending darkness.

Mentally clicking off another day, she sat staring at the two bullets in her other hand. Picking up the fine-point Sharpie she'd been writing in her journal with, she scribbled *I'm done* on one and *Fuck this* on the other. She was too much of a coward for suicide, but she had considered it lately, a lot. Sitting at night in her tent, she could feel the cold steel bump of the 9mm she tucked under her pillow for protection. Now it lay cradled in her lap, the clip pulled out and the bullets scattered around her. She'd even formulated a half-assed plan one night while lying in her sleeping bag.

She could wrap herself in her plastic liner and not make a mess someone else would have to clean up. She'd seal it with duct tape and get inside her sleeping bag, which was in her tent that she would collapse around her for more protection. Then she'd take out her cook pot, place it over her head, and put the gun in her mouth. But which way should she aim the gun? Straight back at her spinal cord or at an angle into her brain? By putting the cook pot over her head, she was certain the bullet wouldn't travel and hurt anyone. She didn't want to be careless with someone else's life.

It wouldn't happen. She was a coward, or maybe just not desperate enough, yet. She could down a fifth of whiskey, which might help facilitate things, but what if she didn't do it? The hangover would be killer.

If she could just reach in and pull the most painful part of her out, she'd be fine. But she suspected her heart wouldn't cooperate with the exorcism. Leaning back against her chair, she twisted her neck and felt the pop. Stress and pain were doing the buddy system in her head. In fact, they were her best friends lately. The beauty of the dusk surrounded her, yet it couldn't find purchase in her soul. Gazing at the night sky, she spotted her first falling star and flung a wish at it. She had given up counting sheep to try to fall asleep. She'd lost so many nights that she dreaded seeing another one fall, but fall they must. Her eyelids drooped and her head finally bobbed backward.

꙰꙰꙰

"Hey, you know the way to the gate?"

The sound of plastic snapping in the breeze caught her attention. The yellow caution tape flapped against the side of a fence. Picking up the end she studied it. CRIME SCENE was printed in big black letters that blocked her path.

"Hey, you know the way to the gate?"

Peering over her left shoulder she saw a young guy, in his mid to late twenties, holding his hand over his chest.

"What gate?'

"*The* gate," he said, staring at her.

"I have no idea what you're talking about," she said, looking around the campsite. Something had happened, but she didn't know what. She also didn't know who this guy was, but she intended to find out.

"What the fuck is going on here?" She stood and looked at him again, noticing his bloody hand covering his chest. "Holy shit, you're bleeding."

"Jesus, you're tall. What are you, about six feet?"

"No. What the hell happened to you?" She

stepped back from the guy, who was definitely in bad shape.

"What?" He pulled his hand away and looked at it. "Oh, this? It happened days ago."

"You need a doctor. Do you have a cell phone? I'd loan you mine, but...but..."

Shit, she hadn't thought about emergencies. What if something had happened to her, what would she do? Who would come to *her* rescue? No one, that's who. No one cared, no one worried about her. She'd go to work, and the same students would be sitting in the same chairs. Their homework wouldn't be done. Her office mate would be bitching about her useless husband, and her boss would ask where her self-evaluation was. No one cared. Especially her cheating girlfriend, Renee. She was the reason she was up here. Fucking bitch.

"Just point me in the direction of the gate, and I'll be out of your hair, lady," he said, looking past her.

Turning, she tried to see what he was looking at, but nothing was behind her.

"Wait. At least let me get my first-aid kit," she said, scrambling to her tent.

He grabbed her arm and stopped her before she got anywhere. "I don't need a doctor. I don't need first aid."

"But—"

"I did this to myself. I don't need help."

"I don't understand," she said, stepping back from him. "How did you do that?" She pointed to his bloody hand.

"I had too much to drink, and pow. Look, I got a shitty life, a shitty job, and I do, correction, did way too many drugs. So, last night I got drunk, said fuck it, and…" He made the shape of a gun with his finger and thumb, then pointed it to his chest. "Pow."

"Oh, my God, you shot yourself. Is the bullet still in there?" She walked toward him and reached for him, but he grabbed her hands before she could touch the wound.

"I get it. You're like that lady in the movie who sees dead people and doesn't even know it."

"What? What are you talking about?"

"I committed suicide, lady." He dropped her hands and looked at her funny. "What'd you do?"

"Do? I…I didn't do anything." She looked around again. She was in her campsite, her stuff still in the same place she'd left it. But the remnants of crime-scene tape flapping in the breeze caught her attention, again. Looking down at her own hands, she realized she was holding something tight in the palm of one of them. Opening it, she saw an empty shell casing fall to the ground, heard the tinkle of bouncing copper echoing in the wind. *Fuck this* was written on the side of the shell.

"What happened?"

"What?" she whispered, staring at the brass beacon of her demise. Opening her hand, she could make out the indention of the casing on her palm, but where was the blood? The guy standing in front of her had blood on his hand, his chest. Hell, he looked like he'd taken a bath in it, but where was hers? She patted her body for a wound but didn't find anything.

"On the side of your head?" he said, reaching up to touch her.

She flinched back out of reach and felt her temple. "Oh God," she whispered. "Oh God, this is just a dream. Oh God, this is just a dream." She kept repeating the words as she walked in circles, waving her hands.

"I don't think so."

"It has to be. I was just sitting there watching the sunset. I wished on the first star and everything."

"You don't remember shooting yourself? Holy shit."

"No, I don't remember anything."

"Seriously? I mean, damn. I remember putting the gun up to my chest, counting to three, and pow. I sat there for a minute, and then boom, I was—"

"Stop, don't say another word. Just stop. I didn't kill myself." She was still wringing her hands, but at least now she was standing still. "I mean I thought about it, had a plan and everything."

"Well, if you ask me, you had more than a plan." He reached down and picked up the bullet casing. "You even wrote *Fuck this* on the bullet you used."

"I did not kill myself. I didn't. I didn't have the gun in my hand. I put it right there under my pillow." She stopped at the opening of her tent and peered inside. Blood soaked her pillow. The cook pot sat next to it with a small dent she could barely make out. "I didn't, I didn't, and I couldn't. I mean, I just..."

He peeked inside the tent, too. "Nope. I'd say you did the deed." He pushed the flap closed and pulled down the zipper. "Look, my sponsor said I'd have a guide to help me get through this. Show me where the gate is and all."

This wasn't happening. She wasn't dead and she didn't commit suicide. She would never let Renee win like that, never. Stepping back, she looked down and noticed the trash left from bandages, IV bags, and medical tubing. A set of tracks led past the crime-scene tape. A new set of tire tracks, probably an ambulance, had driven out and down the road. Lots of footsteps littered the ground. How come she hadn't seen them before?

She looked around for her Willys Jeep, but it was gone too. "What the fuck am I going to do now?"

"Well, if you focus, really focus, you can pop back into your body." He put his hands on her arm and then spoke softly. "I wouldn't do that. I did and was right in the middle of being embalmed. Gross." He shivered, making a face.

"How am I going to get home? My car's gone. I live miles from here, and…I need to go home." She unzipped the tent, fell to her knees, and started to cry. When she picked up her pillow, an empty whiskey bottle rolled away from it. She stared at the bottle and then her blood-soaked pillow. Christ, what had she done?

"What are you doing?"

"Look, I don't know who you are or why you're here—"

"Jack," he said, sticking out his bloody hand.

"I'm not shaking that. It looks like it's still wet." Her stomach lurched as she caught a whiff of the smell.

"Hey. You're one of the few people I've found out here, so we must have met for a reason." Jack tried to wipe his hand on his white T-shirt, but the blood wasn't coming off, only smearing across his shirt.

She stuffed her sleeping bag into her pack, then tossed out her pillow, the tin pot, and everything else into the tent. After breaking it down, she put it into her backpack too. Everything felt real. If she was on a different plane, why could she still pack all this?

"I'm getting the fuck out of here." She slipped

her knife into her jeans pocket. "I have a teaching job to get back to, the semester starts next week and a cheating girlfriend that I need to break up with. So, whatever you got going on here..." She swirled her fingers around. "Doesn't involve me. All this shit, it's just a dream. Why I'd dream this is beyond me. Maybe it's one of those Christmas-ghost kinda things. You know, where they show you what your life would be like if you did something stupid."

Jack shook his head. "What? I know this is all new to you, but you had that shell casing in your hand. The one that said *Fuck this.* You got a hole in your head. Turn around." He put his hands on her shoulders and hesitantly moved her around. "Interesting." He pushed strands of brown hair to the side, looking for something, but she had no clue what he was hunting.

"What?"

"No exit wound."

"What?" She hadn't thought about that. Reaching up, she touched the back of her head. Nothing. No blood, no hole, nothing. "See. Maybe this is just a big dream and you're part of my delusional mind. I don't have time for this crap." She grabbed her gun, loaded it, and shoved it inside her waistband. "I can't believe someone stole my truck. Fuck me."

Pulling bandages from her first-aid kit, she covered the hole in her head. "Can you hold this while I tape it?" She motioned to Jack.

"Sure, but it won't make a difference. I'm telling you dead is dead."

"Just hold this." She removed her hand and pulled strips off the medical tape.

"To be honest, now that I look at it, I'm kinda surprised it isn't bigger. I mean, I saw a guy who shot his head, and the back was blown almost off. Kinda gross."

"Hush." Harley couldn't take any more dead talk. She wasn't dead, period.

After finishing the patch job, she pulled her baseball cap out of her backpack and put it on to hide the bandage well enough that she wouldn't be stared at when she went home.

"Thanks," she told Jack.

After putting all her supplies back into her kit and shoving it into her pack, she hoisted it onto her shoulders. It was going to be a long walk home. Probably take her days, if she didn't get a ride. Pushing past Jack, she stopped with a jerk as a five-point buck stood in her path, piercing her with his gaze. They stared at each other for a long moment, neither moving. She was scared as shit. She could barely breathe, frozen where she stood.

"Jesus," Jack said. "I haven't seen one of these big bastards in years, and now here's one in a face-off with you. Damn." Jack raised his hands, trying to scare the buck off. "Arrgggg," he said, moving toward the massive beast.

Undeterred, the buck stepped toward Harley, sniffing her. She reached out and stroked the enormous rack of horns, and when he dropped his head, she rubbed her fingers across the strong plane of his face. She should be freaked out by the size of the buck, but she felt the need to touch him, to feel his energy. What the fuck was wrong with her, feel his energy? They both calmed at the touch as something passed through her.

She didn't have time to analyze what the hell was going on. She just wanted to get home, pull the covers over her head, and wake the hell up. As if reading her thoughts, the buck jerked his head sideways and roofed the ground, then galloped toward the forest. He stopped, then turned and looked at her one more time before he retreated deeper into the dark, lush green. Christ, could this day get any weirder?

Jack followed Harley as she slung her pack on and started walking. "That was amazing. What do you think was up with all that?"

"Look, don't you need to go find your watcher, or something?"

Her corrected her. "Guardian or guide."

"Whatever, but that isn't me. So if you'll excuse me, I'm going home. I want to wake up from this bullshit."

"Okay, but I'm telling you, you're not going to be able to do anything but come with me and get to the gate."

"I'm not like you. I ain't dead." She shifted her backpack and kept going down the dirt road. "See, I can pick up my stuff. I touched that deer back there, and I'm kicking up dust."

Jack stopped and stood there, a puzzled look on his face. He walked behind her, no dust.

"See," she said, pointing to his feet, which weren't leaving any tracks. "We aren't the same."

"Yeah, but you can see me. I touched you." Jack seemed more than a little puzzled.

She pressed her lips together and shrugged. "Don't know what to tell ya. I'd love to sit here and chat, but I need to be going. Good luck finding that watcher."

"Guardian or guide."

Stopping, she turned back toward him. "You mean like a guardian angel or something?"

"Sorta. My spiritual guide said it would meet me when I crossed over."

"Okay, now I'm really confused. You had a spiritual guide," she asked, making air quotes. "He told you to kill yourself? I thought that was like a sin or something."

"Oh no. He would never have approved of me killing myself." Jack's face colored. "I'd just found out I have cancer, or had cancer, and the prognosis wasn't very good. So I got drunk and bang." He shot his chest again.

"So you were going to die anyway." She shook her head. Christ, and she thought she had it bad.

"No. No, actually I was going to lose my testicles, and with chemo the survivability rate is pretty good."

"What the fuck?"

"Hey, don't mix drinking and losing your manhood all in the same night. I didn't say I was dealing with a full deck at that moment. My buddies tried to stop me, but I was just horsing around and here I am, with you."

"Okay, let's get this straight. We aren't together. You need to go find your gate, and I need to get home and wake up from this damn nightmare. So go."

She shooed him away and started walking down the road again.

Chapter Two

Judging from the sun's location overhead, she figured it had to be close to noon. She'd walked for hours and still didn't see the main road yet. She froze when she looked at her watch. July 23, three days later. Backtracking in her mind, she'd hit the campground late on July 19, pitched her tent, had a drink—okay, a few drinks—and sat wallowing in her hate and denial until she went to sleep.

During a lousy night of tossing and turning, she'd dreamt of her lover and watching her over and over again kissing that bitch she'd spied her with.

She got up, took a piss, and walked the campgrounds. It was too hot for campers, except a few die-hard guys who stayed at the opposite end of the place. From the looks of their camp, they were there to hunt and party, if the empty whiskey bottles and beer cans lying around were any indication. Stepping backward, she retreated the way she'd come and put as much distance between her and them as she could. No use inviting trouble, even if it did seem to have a way of finding her.

How the hell had she lost three days? She reached up and touched the small wound on the side of her head. Something didn't seem right. A 9mm would have created a giant exit wound on the back of her head and the pot. The pot had a dent on the outside instead of the inside. Shit, it didn't make sense.

As she pushed farther down the dirt road, she was determined to at least hit the paved road before dark, hitch a ride, and get the hell home. The beating sun was wearing her out though. Getting off the road, she found some shade and pulled her pack, reaching for a bottle of water. She sipped it. If she were dead, how could she drink water? As soon as the liquid hit her stomach, it growled.

Food.

How many days had she been without food? Didn't people die of dehydration after only a few days? She'd lost three. No food, no water until now, nothing. No matter how she tried to wrap her mind around things, she just couldn't accept the possibility that she'd committed suicide. God, not over Renee.

"Hey, there you are." Jack strolled up and plopped down beside her. "How far do you think you've walked? By the way, you never told me your name."

She refused to look at him. It freaked her out seeing the big hole in his chest and all that blood. Maybe if she ignored him, he'd go away. Please leave me alone, she thought, taking another sip of water.

"I'm not going away. You can drink water?" Jack's laser-like focus on her made her twitch.

"Yep. Proves I'm not dead." She stood and packed her bottle into the side pocket of her backpack and shrugged it on.

"Okay, if you say so, but I'm just sayin'—"

"Stop." She threw up her hands. "Don't you have a gate or something to find?"

"Yeah, but—"

"No buts. I'm not your finder—"

"Guide."

"Whatever, I'm not that person."

"You know what?" Jack crossed his arms and stared right through her. "You're the first person I've found that is like, well, like you."

"What do you mean?"

"You drink, but I don't feel the need to drink. You're hungry. I can touch you. I can't touch other people I've seen. We just, whoosh," he said, pushing his hands past each other. "It's like those ghost movies you've seen on TV. Spirits can't touch, except the bad ones."

"Bad ones? What the fuck are you talking about?"

"I call 'em Dark Souls. You know, those people who can go through the gate." Jack looked around and then lowered his head and whispered into her ear. "They wanna kill us."

"Okay, now you're freaking me out." She put her hands up and pushed him back to clear her path. "I don't know anything about gates, Dark Souls, or spirits. Hell, I don't even believe in God."

"You don't have to believe in God to see this shit. Tell me this. Why are you and I having a conversation?" He raised his eyebrows in question.

"I'm dreaming and you're part of my damn nightmare. No offense, but I'm sure when I wake up, I'll need to see a counselor or something to sort this shit out." She pushed through some bushes. "Now if you'll excuse me, I need to pee."

"I'll just wait right here for you," Jack said, sitting down. "Besides, I'm not feeling well." He twisted his head and then rubbed his stomach.

Harley watched him through the bushes, drawing in the dirt. He could touch the dirt, but nothing moved. She'd seen him lean against a tree, but he didn't go through it.

"How come you can sit on the ground or you could lean against that tree over there when we were talking?"

"I can walk through it if you want me to."

"Nope. Just thinking out loud."

"I don't know. I just can."

"Hmm."

Nothing made sense in this dream, nothing. Zipping up her pants, she walked out of the bushes and headed away from Jack.

"Well, until I wake up, I'm going in the direction of home."

"Wait. Who's going to help me find the gate?"

"Don't know."

"Wait," he said, pulling on her arm.

"Don't touch me." Harley shook him off.

"Sorry." Jack took a step back. "There are people out there who can hurt us, I mean you, so you should be careful."

Harley patted her waistband, her 9mm lodged securely there. Pulling it, she dropped the clip and checked it. "Hmm, nine shots, so I don't think so."

Jack rubbed the back of his neck and made a face. "Yeah. I'm not sure that's gonna work."

"Let me ask you something completely off the subject."

"Okay." Jack looked down at the dirt, twisting his toe into it. Suddenly he looked embarrassed. Why?

"Where did you kill yourself?"

"Oh, um." He threw his hand over his shoulder, pointing his thumb behind him. "Over off Lexington in Gilroy. My apartment is 1438 North—"

Harley held up her hands, stopping him. "I don't need to know the address. How did you get here?" She pointed to the ground. "That's what, two hours away, driving?"

"Yeah."

"So you mean to tell me you walked, what, a day, day and a half, to get all the way out here?"

"Not exactly."

She eyed him suspiciously. He wasn't telling her something. He didn't walk here. He said he'd committed suicide in his apartment with his buddies sitting around him. Yet he was here.

"How did you get here?"

"Well, I just was…" He stopped and looked around again.

What or whoever he was looking for was making her nervous. "Was what?"

"I just thought, where would the gate be? Then I figured it was some place in nature, probably hidden away in some forest. You know, like in those movies where the secret door is in some rocks or something like that. So I imagined the forest, and bam. Here I am."

"So you just imagine some place, like when you wanted to find your body, and you're there?"

"Something like that." Jack blushed.

Harley closed her eyes tight and imagined her house. Nothing.

"What are you doing?"

"I'm thinking about home. I want to go home."

"But you're still here."

"No shit, Captain Obvious."

Harley started walking again. She definitely wasn't dead. However, that didn't explain how she could talk to Jack, assuming he was the only one. She was definitely dreaming.

Chapter Three

Hey, wait up," Jack screamed at her.
"Jack, go find your gate. I'm not your keeper. Leave me alone."

Harley had enough problems. Being someone's keeper wasn't on her list of job duties, and she wasn't picking up any strays. She pushed farther ahead until a hand on her shoulder stopped her.

"Hey, girl, listen to me."

Harley flinched. "I'm not a girl. I'm a grown-ass woman."

"Well, you still haven't told me your name, so until then it's whatever I call you."

"Really?"

Jack had suddenly grown some balls. Or had they been there the whole time and he was just being polite earlier because he thought she was his finder? Guardian, or whatever.

"Harley, my name is Harley."

"Like the motorcycle?" Jack said, making throttle signals with his hands and sputtering his lips.

"My dad loves motorcycles, and I happened to be stuck with the name. I was supposed to be a boy," she said, her voice flat.

"Ah, gotcha."

She turned and continued down the road. The sounds of traffic off in the distance spurred her to walk faster. Running wasn't an option. Her head was suddenly killing her. What she wouldn't do for some aspirin.

"Hey, wait, Harley."

"Jack," she screamed. "Go find your keeper and leave me the fuck alone."

"Guide, Harley. Guide."

"Whatever."

"Stop."

"Fuck," she said under her breath. He was never going to leave her alone, was he?

"It's not safe out there."

"What are you talking about? This…" She twirled her fingers, pointing toward the sky. "This is all a dream. So get out of my head and leave me alone."

"Harley, I've seen some stuff on this side, and you aren't safe."

"Oh, my God, are you kidding me right now?" Looking around, she yelled, "Okay, you've punked me. I get that I'm on camera. The head wound, this guy, it's all been fun, but you can come out now. It isn't funny." She looked around, waiting for someone to appear out of nowhere and tell her it was all a big joke at her expense.

Silence.

"Are you done?" Jack stepped closer. "What's the date today?"

"What?"

"What's the date today?"

She knew what the date was, but she looked at her watch for confirmation. "July 23."

"I've been dead for over six months."

"I thought…" Harley looked at Jack's gaping chest wound and then back to his face. "I don't understand. I thought you said you just did this?"

He shook his head. "I've been looking for the gate for six months. I've seen things here…" He stopped and scrunched his face, his bottom lip starting to quiver.

She couldn't stand to see a grown man cry, so she did the only thing she knew to do. Run.

She put as much distance between her and Jack as she could. Something wasn't right here, and she wasn't sticking around to find out what.

"Harley, wait."

Suddenly Jack was standing in front of her, stopping her.

"What the fuck. How did you do that?"

"Listen to me." He put his hands on her shoulders and held her firm. "I've tried to tell you that something's going on, but you're not listening. There are people out here who want us dead."

"Dark Souls," she stated for confirmation.

"Gatekeepers."

Harley threw up her hands and covered her ears. "Blah, blah, blah. I'm not listening. I'm not being sucked into someone else's dream."

Jack jerked her hands down. "Stop acting like a child and listen to me. I don't care what you think, but you're here now. I don't know what you are or how you got here, but you're going to have to accept this as your new reality. Do you understand?"

"I'm telling you that I'm going to wake up and it's all going to be a nightmare. You'll be gone—this bullshit will be gone. I'll go back to my crappy life teaching college and to a cheating girlfriend—who I'll promptly break up with and then get on with my life."

"Shh." He clasped his hand over her mouth.

She could feel him willing her to shut up.

Chapter Four

I felt the little bastard somewhere around here," a tall, skinny man said.

"Yeah, probably long gone. I checked the campsite where that bitch was, and she's gone, too. Think they left together?" another man asked.

Something about these guys gave Harley the willies. Something was wrong with the skinny man's face, and the other guy, well, he looked like death warmed over. Cliché, but she couldn't think of any other way to describe him.

"Dark Souls?" Harley whispered.

Jack put his finger to his lips. "Shh."

"Well, I don't feel him around here, so the little prick must have gotten away," the skinny man said, turning in circles. "Let's go back and catch that chick by the pond. She won't see it coming."

"Yeah, but can we have a little fun with her before we dispatch her?"

Harley's heart raced as she wondered who they were talking about. She started to stand, but Jack held her down and shook his head. He signaled for her to wait, never taking his eyes off the pair. She looked back at them just in time to see nothing but some dark mist left in their wake.

"What the fuck?" She ran to where they'd stood and swished her hand around. The heat of the mist burned her. "Ouch."

"Now do you believe me?" Jack started walking in circles around the area they'd been, not touching the black fog that lingered.

"Gatekeepers?"

"Sorta. They think they keep the balance. Too many can't go through the gate. At least they don't want too many going through it. They think it's their job to keep inventory of those that do."

"What?"

"I can't explain it. It isn't just a matter of finding the gate. You have to get past these guys, and that's the problem. Dark Souls."

"What about that woman they were talking about? It doesn't sound like they're just going to kill her. It sounded more like they were going to...I don't know...torture or rape her?"

"Maybe."

"You say that like it's no big deal. Really?"

"Look, I'm just trying to get to the gate. I'm not responsible for anyone else and how they get there."

"Hold on. You were just trying to get me to take you to the gate, and now you're telling me you're not responsible for anyone else?"

"Yeah, that's sorta how it works out here."

At least Jack had the decency to look ashamed.

"But they work in teams, so why can't you and another person do that?"

"Did you hear what he said? He said he could smell me, so how do you think they track us? The more people together, the bigger the stench."

"So why didn't he smell you now?"

Jack shrugged. "YOU!" he said. "It has to be you. Whatever's going on with you, you're the one masking my smell."

"Oh no. I'm not getting sucked further into this mess. I'm not a protector or something."

"You're already in this mess. You heard them say they saw you earlier. What was that all about?"

"I don't have a clue, and I'm not sticking around to find out." Harley pushed past Jack and continued down the dirt road. A flash of a girl sitting near water popped in her head. Somehow Harley knew this girl wouldn't see them coming. Running back to Jack, she grabbed his arm. "You need to get to that girl. You need to warn her."

"Did you just hear what I said? They'll smell us. She's sure as dispatched if I show up."

"She's dispatched if you don't. Don't you care? Isn't that part of your reason for finding the gate, 'cause you're a good person?"

Harley didn't know how any of this crap worked, but she was sure only truly good people passed through the gate. At least she hoped that was how it operated.

"You help her. I need to find the gate and get to the other side."

"Me? Do you see me walking? I don't seem to be able to…" She hit the tree, a resounding thud her point. "I can't move through things. I'm stuck walking home, but you, you can walk through shit. You can imagine a place and be there. Me, I'm just here," she said, lifting her hands and shrugging.

"I wouldn't begin to know where to look for her."

"She's by some water," Harley said.

"How do you know?"

"I saw her, it just flashed. Ducks, forest, shit like that are all around her."

"She's hiding?"

"Probably." Harley had another flash of memory.

A brunette sitting behind a tree holding something. Jeans, a corded sweater, and her hair up in a ponytail. "She's scared. You have to do something, Jack."

"I can't."

"You selfish prick."

"Yeah, well, better to be alive in this space than dispatched."

"Jesus, you're a king-size asshole." Harley started running for the road, the thud of her steps heavy behind her as she darted for the line of trees along the road. How was she going to get home, or to the woman and warn her?

"Harley, wait." Jack stood next to her.

"Cut that out. You scared the shit out of me. Why don't you disappear and find that gate you're looking for?"

"Maybe we can help each other?"

"How?"

"We find the girl, you help me find the gate, and we call it even?"

"I. Don't. Know. Where. The. Gate. Is. Don't you understand?"

Jack hung his head. "Yeah, but maybe—"

"No maybes, Jack. I have no idea."

"Listen, if I can jump...maybe if I hold your hand, you can make the jump too." Jack held out his hand, waiting.

Harley looked at it.

"It's your only chance at maybe, just maybe, getting to this woman first. Besides, if they couldn't smell me out here, maybe you can mask her smell, too."

"Shit." Harley shrugged again. What other strange stuff could happen to her today? "Fuck." She hesitated, not wanting to take his hand. "Wait. We aren't going to end up in some cemetery or some shit, are we?"

"Think about where you saw her. Focus on that, and I'll try to focus on the same thing. You said she was by some water, ducks, and trees. Right?"

"Yep."

"Okay, let's do this."

Harley grabbed his hand and stiffened at the contact. A surge split through her and her mind went dark.

Chapter Five

"Harley. Harley. Wake up."

Her body shook, and then someone pulled her arm, sitting her upright. Her headache, which never really went away, was worse. When she touched her bandage, blood moistened her fingertips.

"Shit," she said, looking at her hand. Her left side felt like little daggers were stabbing her. The tingling that came with that kind of numbness hurt like hell. Pushing Jack's hands away, she said, "Don't touch me."

She crawled to her knees, steadying herself. She was looking through a tunnel, the black edges receding slowly, opening up her view of the world around her. The forest was dark, foreboding and ominous. The canopy of trees barely let any light down to the floor below. The musty smell of decomposing leaves and whatever lived in there was so overpowering, she thought she might puke.

Clutching her head, she stayed on her knees. She swayed and then grabbed the floor for purchase, trying to keep from tumbling over.

"Are you okay?" Jack knelt next to her, his hand on her back rubbing it.

"Find the girl. I'll be fine." Harley's throat tightened and her stomach started to jerk, ready to expel the water she'd had earlier. "Christ. Is this normal?"

"I gotta tell you, I'm surprised I could get you

here." Jack sprouted a smirk. Clearly, he was pretty proud of himself and what he'd done.

"Find that woman and be careful. We don't know where those Dark Souls are, or if they're even here."

"I'm not going without you. It's pretty evident that they can't get a bead on me when you're around, so I'm staying right here." Jack sat next to her.

"Jeez. A spirit with no balls."

"No. I just want to make it to the gate in one piece."

Harley twisted around to her knees again and stuck her hand out. "Help me get up, please."

Jack pulled her to her feet and caught her just as she was about to topple over. "I gotcha."

"Thanks."

"I don't know what just happened, but I'm not sure I can do that again." Harley clutched her stomach.

"You get used to it...eventually."

"I don't want to get used to it. I just want to go home, wake up, and forget this dream." Harley brushed dead debris from her knees, looked around, and started walking.

"Where are you going?" Jack, as usual, was playing catch-up to Harley's lead.

"To find that chick."

"Chick? You don't even know where she is, right?"

Harley pushed farther along the tree line, trying to stay out of sight. The sound of ducks echoed in the distance. Moving faster, she felt panic grip her. What if they couldn't find the girl in time? What would happen to her? She'd die. At least that was what Jack had said. What happened to souls that did find the gate? It didn't matter. She'd seen this woman—a premonition she couldn't explain.

"There," Harley said, pointing to something across the lake.

A woman sat looking at the ducks, just like in her dream.

"Shit, we need to hurry. I can feel them," Jack said, taking off in an all-out sprint.

Harley tried to follow, but a bass drum was beating inside her skull. "Go. I'll follow. Just get to her." Harley had pushed farther, still following the tree line, when she heard a man's voice somewhere behind her.

"Hey, there's that bitch we've been after. She's just there like a sittin' duck." He laughed.

Another voice boomed behind her. "Who's that guy running toward her? Oh, man, that's that Jack guy. He is so dead."

Turning, she expected the men to see her, but they stood right behind her as if she didn't exist. She crinkled her nose at the stench coming off the man whose face was, upon closer inspection, decaying. Death. That's what death must smell like when a corpse started rotting. Her lip quivered. Her stomach rolled. She bit her tongue, trying to control the heave that was threatening.

"We need to kill them before they get to the gate," Dead Face said.

Harley stood behind as they passed her by. She needed to do something, but what? The only thing she could think of was tucked into the waist of her pants. She pulled the hammer back on her gun, ran up to the man trailing behind Dead Face, stopped, pulled the trigger, and shot him in the head. Seeming stunned, Dead Face stood still, his eyes following his buddy's body as it dropped to the ground.

"What the fuck?" In that brief moment, he must have seen her.

Like a movie that had suddenly been kicked into slow motion, he reached for her. She twisted to the left, raised her gun again, and fired. This time, the bullet passed by her target as he lunged in her direction. A quick step back and he was grasping where she had been only a second earlier. Swinging his arms widely, he tried to find her, but it was like he was blind.

"Where the fuck are you, bitch?"

He stepped in the opposite direction of where she stood. Something wasn't right. He'd seen her for a split second, and now he acted as if she were gone. Whatever happened, she wasn't sticking around to find out why he couldn't see her. She needed to get to the woman and Jack before this guy put two and two together.

Racing toward Jack, she screamed at him to run. Jack and the woman just stood there frozen. They had to have at least heard the gunshot, right? Jack pointed to her and screamed something. Too far away to hear anything, she had just enough time to look behind her. Dead Face was heading at her in a full charge.

Chapter Six

"Damn it. Run, Jack," she said under her breath. She didn't take her eyes off the pair as they headed into the trees. Harley pushed herself, running with the gun in hand, then turned to fire. Dead Face was gone. *What the hell?*

Not waiting to find out what had happened, Harley pushed her body. Her headache was back, only this time she could barely focus on anything. Stumbling toward the trees, she decided they were her only chance to hide. The coolness of the shade the forest offered and the smell of decomposing leaves signaled she'd found refuge. Reaching around, she touched the rough bark of a tree. Now crawling on her hands and knees, she sat against it and waited. She could barely make out the light and shadows, so she listened.

Nothing. No birds, no ducks, not even the rustle of leaves in the breeze. Harley pulled the gun against her chest. The thud of footsteps in the leaves made her turn. Pulling back the hammer, she waited.

"I heard it come from over here. Oh, shit, what is that smell?" a low baritone whispered.

"Look, it's a Dark Soul. There. Someone shot him."

"Don't touch him. He'll burn you."

"He's dead."

"Doesn't matter. I've seen the damage they can do even dead."

Harley could barely make out their shadows, and just as she was about to make her presence known she heard the second one say, "They roam in pairs. We better get out of here. The other one is probably still around."

Frozen against the tree, she released the breath she was holding. What the hell was going on? These guys couldn't kill the Dark Souls, but she could. Nothing made sense.

"Who do you think did this?"

"I don't know. I didn't know you could kill them."

"Great. Now we have something even worse than a Dark Soul to worry about?"

"Get back into the trees, and let's see if we can find the others. We've got to find the gate."

She watched as they disappeared into the dark shadows of the forest. She had to hide, but she could barely move. She was a target as long as she stayed there. Pushing up against the tree, she grasped it for support. Then she put her back against a tree again and did her best to survey her surroundings. It was clear Jack wasn't coming back and she was on her own. Probably best that way since he was keeping her from going home. *God.* Now she was thinking this was reality. A branch broke somewhere close to her. She stiffened. Pushing off the tree, she moved deeper into the darkness. Out in the light, she had a big target on her back. At least in here, she could seep into the deepest recesses and hide.

A nudge in her back made her freeze. Fast, quick breaths pelted her neck.

"Christ," she said, pulling her gun into her chest. If she turned and fell backward, she could get a shot off. Assuming he stayed where he was, of course.

Another nudge, this one harder, almost pushed her off her feet. She landed on her knees, fell to her side, and pointed her gun above her. She wasn't going down without a fight. She stared as she recognized the giant buck looming over her. Her body melted into the ground, her eyes rolled back, and the world went dark.

Chapter Seven

Her eyes were ocean blue, clear fathomless pools of water that Harley wanted to swim in. The slight smile the woman offered disappeared as quickly as it had surfaced. Everything about her was effervescent. A warm feeling flowed off her and settled into Harley.

This must be what meeting an angel feels like. Harley reached out to touch the woman's hand, but it was pulled back before she could make contact.

"You won't be able to touch me," she said.

Jack voice cut through the moment. "She can touch us. I saw her kill a Dark Soul."

The woman looked up at him and then back at Harley, as Harley shrugged.

"Don't ask me why I can touch you guys," she said, reaching for the woman's hand again. As she ran her fingertips across the back of the stranger's hand, energy surged through Harley. Her mind went places it hadn't in years. She must be sexually frustrated. She hadn't been intimate with a woman for quite some time, but this one wasn't any woman, really. She wasn't even real, as far as Harley could decipher, but more of a wandering soul. Right?

"See." Harley smiled.

Their gaze met, and the woman looked down at her hand, threading her fingers through Harley's. "Amazing."

"Kinda," Harley said and let go of the woman's grasp. She was hungry for something more, but it would only confuse her to get touchy-feely at this moment. "I can't explain it, so don't ask." Harley sat up and hugged her knees tight. "I'm hungry," she said, her usual quick-change artistry at work. "By the way, what's your name?"

"Dawn," the stranger said softly.

"Dawn." Harley let the name linger on her lips. It fit her. Something about the name rang familiar to Harley, yet she couldn't say why. She'd think about it later, when she had time. Now she needed something to eat and someplace safe to hide.

"I'm starving." Harley extended her hand toward Jack.

Jack reached down and pulled Harley to her feet. "Well, don't look at us. We don't have anything for you to eat." He grabbed her backpack and shoved it at her. "Maybe you have some of those nasty protein bars in your pack."

"What's got your panties so bunched up?" Harley riffled through her pack and pulled a smashed, half-eaten candy bar out. "This'll do for now," she said, picking lint off the exposed end.

"Gross. You're not going to eat that?" Jack scrunched his nose.

"Seriously? You're not about to question my food choices, are you?" She peeled the paper off the end of the bar and bit it. "Shit, chocolate never tasted so good." She rolled her eyes and smacked her lips.

"Can we please go?" Looking determined, Jack walked off in the opposite direction of Harley's destination.

"Wait, where are you going?"

"To find the gate, remember?"

"No, no, no, no. Just wait a minute. I need to get home. I need to find out what the hell is going on here." Harley was defiant, putting her hands on her hips. She meant business, and Jack wasn't about to change her plans.

"Look, those Dark Souls are around here somewhere, and I don't want to be here when they show back up. They're searching for you and I saw what you just did to them back there."

Dawn looked back and forth between them, not saying a word. Despondent was the only word Harley could think of as she studied Dawn. There was something calming about her, though. Harley couldn't describe it any other way. Perhaps it was the way an old soul felt. She'd met people who were older than their years, and that's what Dawn reminded her of.

"Jack, I don't know how all this works. I'm not even sure you're real, so bear with me. I need to either wake the fuck up or find out where I am. Now, you can come with me and I can protect you two and figure this all out. Or I can go on my merry way. It's up to you."

Jack threw his hands up. He clearly wasn't happy about the proposition, but then neither was she. It was the best she could do at the moment.

"Fine, but I've already told you, you're dead." Walking past her, he grabbed her hand and pulled her along. Dawn stood where she was rooted. "Aren't you coming?" Jack's impatience was like a lit fuse. He could go off at any minute, and Harley didn't want him combusting all over Dawn, so Harley grabbed her hand and brought her with them.

"Jack. I want you to take me home. You know, pop me back to where my body is right now." The emotion she felt wasn't reflected in her voice. In fact, her emotions were all over the place, and it was all she could do at this very moment not to break down and lose it.

"I told you that probably wasn't a good idea. I mean, remember what happened to me when I did that?"

His body wriggled. She remembered what he'd said about popping into the mortuary and watching them embalm his body. She wasn't dead, though. Harley didn't know how she knew it. She just did.

"Take me home. Now." The tone was harsher than she wanted, but she needed to make a point. She wanted to see for herself and convince him she wasn't dead. Hell, she wanted to convince herself she wasn't dead.

"What's in it for me?"

Harley jerked him to a stop. She'd stubbed the dirt with the toe of her boot kicking up dust. She didn't have anything to bargain with, at least nothing she was willing to do for him.

"I won't kill you."

"What? That's all you got. You won't kill me? Oh, that's good. What makes you think you can kill me?"

"You saw what I did earlier to Dead Face's buddy." Making a gun with her fingers, she held it to her head and popped her thumb down. "Pow." Her hand recoiled in a mock firing.

"You wouldn't."

No, truthfully she wouldn't, but he didn't need to know. She gave him her best deadpan look, crossed her arms, and said, "Try me."

Jack suddenly disappeared. Poof, he was gone.

"Shit." Looking around, she expected to see him

at a distance from her, but he wasn't anywhere. "Geez, I wouldn't kill you, Jack. You big jerk," she said. Waiting for him to reappear, she stamped her foot. "Jack."

Nothing.

She and Dawn exchanged glances and waited a few more minutes. For a soul looking for the gate, he sure was oversensitive. She was wasting time here. She needed to get back fast and find out what was really happening, so she started walking toward what she hoped was home. Her mind couldn't wrap itself around the events of the last few hours. It had been hours, hadn't it? Looking at her watch, she saw it had been only four hours since she'd woken up, or was this a dream? Hell, she didn't know, but she needed answers. The faster she walked the warmer she got. The noonday sun beat down on her.

"For someone who isn't supposed to be alive, I'm sure hot, hungry, and cranky."

"Maybe you're not dead yet," Dawn said.

"That's what I've been saying to Jack. I'm not dead."

Dawn shrugged and walked beside Harley, companionable silence passing between them. Harley didn't know what to say to someone like Dawn. Jack had made it easy. She couldn't shut him up. But Dawn…Dawn was different. Almost ethereal.

Harley pulled her baseball cap off and wiped at the sweat beading on her forehead. Absentmindedly, she ran her fingers through the dark locks, getting them caught in the bandage on the side of her head. Her stride never wavered as she jerked at the medical tape. Pulling strands of hair with it, she worked the tape loose. She tugged the bandage free and studied it. The bloodstain was dark and no longer fresh. Gingerly, she touched around the wound on her head. She wanted to stick her fingers in it but couldn't. So she touched around the edges. A scab was beginning to form. That didn't happen if you were dead, did it? She picked at the caked, dried blood on her face. After drawing out her water bottle, she took a swig and then wet the sleeve of her shirt to wipe the blood off her face. At least she hoped it was only blood.

"Oh, wow. That looks..." Dawn pressed her fingers to her hips, a grimace replacing the stoic look she'd been carrying around.

"Bad? I haven't seen it. I can only touch it." Harley poked around the edges, each time venturing closer to the gaping hole.

"I've seen worse, but yeah. It's pretty gross." Dawn touched Harley's temple.

The softness of her touch exploded through Harley. Goose bumps burst throughout her body. Closing her eyes, she reveled in the feelings. *She's an angel. That's all there is to it.*

"Who are you?" Harley ventured an obvious question. She looked Dawn over and didn't see any signs of trauma. Unlike Jack with his humongous hole in his chest, Dawn was...pristine. Her eyes were the only things that reflected anything back to Harley. *The eyes are the windows to the soul, aren't they?* Isn't that what she'd heard? Well, Dawn's were magnetic, and Harley couldn't figure out why she was so drawn to the woman.

"Dawn, you don't have any signs of trauma, and you don't look sick. Not that I've seen a lot of..." Harley twirled her hand in the air. "Dead people. I mean, well, you know what I mean."

Dawn flashed a small smile and then turned away.

"We should probably get going. I think our safest bet is to walk in the trees. Don't you?"

"Yeah. That's what I was just thinking. Come on. The sooner I get home, the sooner we can figure out what's going on."

Without thinking, Harley grabbed Dawn's hand. Trying to ignore the energy they were sharing, Harley pulled Dawn along, then stopped. "Hold on. If Jack can pop in and out, can you?"

Dawn stuttered for a moment and then bit her lip. Looking everywhere but at Harley, she finally confessed. "I can, yes."

"Then why are we walking?"

"I've never taken someone with me when I jump."

"Have you ever jumped?"

"A few times."

Harley furrowed her eyebrows. Something seemed off about Dawn's answer, but she was in a hurry, and nothing in this world surprised her.

"Okay, so if I imagine it, can you get us there?"

Dawn casually shrugged and then looked past Harley toward something behind her.

"So, I imagined seeing you. Don't you think that's odd? I mean, I don't know you, but I had a premonition. I told Jack. He jumped us here."

Dawn shrugged again, offered a slight smile, and then grabbed Harley's hand. "Okay, let's try it."

"Wait." Harley let Dawn's hand go and threw hers up. "Let me think about this. My body isn't going to be at home. Right?" she said, not expecting an answer. "So, I must be at the hospital. There are only two close to the campground. It must be Clearwater General." She grabbed Dawn's hand, squeezed it, and said, "Go."

Nothing happened. Harley opened her eyes and

looked at Dawn, who was biting her lower lip and looking at Harley.

"What?"

Dawn started to say something, stopped, and then looked down at the ground.

Harley gently yanked her hand. "You don't like hospitals? Okay, then how about you just get me outside and I'll go in by myself?"

Dawn still didn't look at Harley.

"Look, the faster we get this done the faster I can figure out what the hell's going on." Harley lifted Dawn's chin and looked at her. Something was gravely wrong. Harley didn't know what, but she felt it. "What is it?"

⊗⊗⊗⊗

"What's wrong?" Harley demanded. "We don't have time to play coy, so tell me what the fuck is going on."

Fear coursed through Harley. She dropped Dawn's hand and stepped back. Whatever Dawn was feeling, so was Harley. Nothing made sense. Why couldn't she get the answers she needed?

Without thinking, she grabbed Dawn by the shoulders and shook her. "What aren't you telling me? Talk to me, damn it."

"The hospitals are kill zones."

"What?" Harley searched Dawn's face for some emotion, some meaning, but it was hiding. Terror split through Harley's body. She had nothing to be afraid of, so it had to be coming from Dawn. "I can feel you, can't I?"

A puzzled look crossed Dawn's face before she

replaced it with her usual stoic gaze.

"You don't understand anything, do you?"

Now it was Harley's turn to be puzzled. "Did I miss an orientation or something? 'Cause I have no idea what's going on, what the fuck I'm doing here, or who you or Jack are, so yes, I mean no, I don't understand what's going on." Harley stumbled over words that were barely finding a home on her tongue. "What do you mean, the hospitals are kill zones?"

Dawn looked around before she started hoofing it toward the trees. Harley struggled to keep up. Her energy was failing and she needed to eat, or something needed to happen so she could get to the hospital.

"Stop, where are you going?"

"To hide. I'm a target standing out there in the open, and that dead-face guy, as you call him, he's going to be back. This time he'll have a new partner, and they'll be looking for you and Jack. Anyone they can kill because it's what they do." Dawn leaned against a tree, searching the forest ahead.

"They can't see me," she told Dawn. "And they can't smell you as long as you're with me. Jack and I found that out back by my camp."

"It's not me I'm worried about."

Harley shrugged. "I have no idea how this stuff works, but Jack and I were only a few feet from those two dead souls. They couldn't smell him. When I killed that one guy, he dropped like a rock. He didn't even see it coming. The other guy, it looked like he saw me for a few seconds, and then he couldn't see me again. He swung wild when he was trying to hit me, but I dodged him."

"Interesting." Dawn's gaze was still roaming the forest, but she still didn't look at Harley.

"Look, I'm sorry about back there. I shouldn't have put my hands on you, but I'm feeling a little desperate right now. I need to get to the hospital and see what's going on. I'm not dead. I'm not."

"No, you're definitely not dead."

"So, if I can protect you at the hospital, can you get me there? Please?" Harley wasn't above begging at the moment. Time seemed to be wasting away and she needed answers.

Dawn grabbed Harley's hand and squeezed it. "We can give it a try. I'm putting my safety in your hands."

"I'll protect you." Harley didn't know if she could keep that promise, but she'd die trying. "Okay, ready when you are," she said, squeezing her eyes shut.

Chapter Eight

M achines buzzed, people scurried around the ICU floor, and Harley and Dawn stood in the middle of the action. They had forgotten all about Jack. Harley searched around, but she didn't see him anywhere. Hell, served him right. He could have helped her, but he'd bailed when she needed him to do her a solid. Didn't matter to her. She wasn't keen on the idea of helping him anyway. Without notice, two Dark Souls walked right past her and Dawn and into a room. An automated code blue was called out to the room they entered. Nurses scrambled, pushing a crash cart into it.

"Clear," someone yelled.

Thump, thump.

"Clear," the voice said again.

Thump, thump.

Beep, beep—followed by a long buzz sounding in the room.

"One more time."

Thump, thump.

The continuous beep of a flat line sounded. The Dark Souls walked out of the room, smiling and high-fiving each other.

"Another one bites the dust," one said in a sing-song voice as he clapped his hands together, motioning as if wiping them clean. "Let's see. Shall we check in on that baby in the NICU? She's looking a bit pale."

"Okay, but this time I get to do the honors."

Harley positioned herself between the men and Dawn. Pulling her gun, she eased the hammer back and waited. If she were wrong, she'd only have a minute at most to kill them. If she missed, Dawn would pay the price, not her.

"Do you smell that?"

Harley flinched, her gun pointed at the man closest to her. These guys didn't look anything like Dead Face. Average Joes, so to speak.

"Naw. I don't smell nothin'."

"Hmm, okay. Well, off to the NICU then. This is getting too easy."

"Yeah. I know what you mean. There's no sport in it anymore." One laughed and slapped the other on the back.

Harley knew one way to end the sport. Heaving her gun up, she shot one and watched him fall. Just as she was aiming at the other, he spotted her and lunged for her. She tried to step back. Dawn, who was standing behind Harley, stopped her, and they both fell to the ground with Harley on top of Dawn, the Dark Soul on top of Harley.

"You fucking little bitch. Who the fuck are you?" He stretched his hands around her neck and started choking her, then spotted Dawn under Harley. "You! We've been looking all over for you, Dawn."

Harley could feel her very existence being sucked out of her. She wanted answers, but she was fighting for her life. Before the guy could say another word, Harley put the gun to his head and pulled the trigger.

Bam.

Black fog replaced the man's image. She remembered one of the Dark Soul's saying it could burn them, so she quickly turned and covered Dawn face from the sizzling mist.

"You killed them," Dawn whispered, surprise evident in her voice.

"Yeah. I guess I did." Harley rose on her elbows and looked at Dawn. God, she was beautiful. Harley let her thumb caress the soft angle of her jaw, and then, without warning, she kissed Dawn. Soft, full lips pressed back.

In a normal world, they would be making a scene, sort of. Harley shivered. She wasn't in her world and they couldn't risk lying on the ground. Other Dark Souls might be flitting around somewhere. Lifting herself off, she looked at Dawn again.

"Tell me what's going on, please," Harley said, pulling Dawn to her feet. "How does he know who you are?" Harley pulled them along the hallway and into a closet. "Great. I worked so hard to get out of the closet, and here I am again." She chuckled at her lame joke.

Harley wrestled with what she needed most—either answers or finding out what was going on with her body. She crossed her arms and waited. Staring at Dawn, she suddenly felt the need to take her in her arms and kiss her again. *Christ, what is wrong with me?*

A stab of pain lanced through her temple. "Argh." She fell to her knees, doubling over. "Jesus."

"Harley, what's wrong?" Dawn knelt beside her.

"My head, it's splitting open."

Harley curled tighter into herself. The pain was unbearable. Light pierced her skull. Then she heard a voice.

"Harley, this is Doctor Millsap. Can you open your eyes for me?"

"What the fuck's going on?" She squeezed her

eyes tighter, trying to keep the light out.

"Harley, honey. It's me, Renee. Come on, baby. Open your eyes."

She couldn't believe Renee had the nerve to talk to her after what she'd done. Where was that bitch? Harley needed to give her a piece of her mind.

Chapter Nine

Harley threw her arm over her eyes, hoping it would block out the nauseating pain. Lying on her back, she felt Dawn's hands on her stomach. Warm energy vibrated through her body.

"Harley, focus on my voice," Dawn whispered close to her ear. "I want you to listen. You need to relax. You're standing between this world and your world."

"What?" Harley tried to look at Dawn, who had a blinding blue aura swimming around her. Shading her eyes, Harley squinted. "Who are you?"

"I'm just here to help."

"Help with what?" Harley's head was exploding, and fireworks were going off behind her closed eyes. "Can you turn the frickin' light show off? It's killing me."

"Harley, can you move your fingers for me?" a man's voice said off in the distance.

"Who is that?" she asked.

"That's the doctor in your room, Harley. Can you get up?" Dawn pulled her arm.

If she didn't know better she would have thought she'd been on a three-day bender. The landscape spun and she weaved. Trying to right herself, Harley gripped the floor, her stomach starting the lurching dance so often associated with one of her few drunken sprees.

"Harley, I'm going to put my hands on your head. Don't move."

Suddenly, the pain disappeared. Harley looked at Dawn, whose eyes were closed, her lips moving, but nothing came out. Was she chanting? No, she was praying. What the hell was going on?

Harley reached up and put her hands on Dawn's and removed them from her head.

"Thanks, it's gone. What the hell?"

"It's hard to explain." Dawn stood and brushed something off her pants.

"Try me." Harley stood, still wobbly. "Are you an…" She wasn't sure she could bring herself to say it, but clearly she was the only one without a clue. "An angel or something? I mean, if those guys out there are Dark Souls," she made air quotes, "then there have to be light souls. Right?"

"Sort of."

"Look. I'm not going to sit here and flirt it out of you. What are you? What am I doing here?"

"Maybe we should go in and check on your body." Dawn pulled the door and peeked out into the hallway. "Come on."

"Why do you know where I am in this place?"

"Just a hunch."

"Somehow I doubt it." Harley snuck a quick look for herself before she followed Dawn. She wasn't about to walk into something. But what was that *something,* now that she thought about it? The hell if she knew, but nothing was adding up, and she considered herself pretty good at math.

Rushing down the halls, Dawn stopped and pointed to a room in ICU. "In there."

Tentatively, Harley looked through the window into the intensive care unit. She expected to see nurses scurrying around, yet only a few casually chatted at the nurses' station. A bank of monitors displayed the vital signs of the patients in all ten rooms. The bright, sterile walls reflected the fluorescent lights, further brightening the room. An alarm went off, and all the nurses rushed to room six, where a hysterical woman was rushed out of the room. Harley caught sight of a flash of black before she ducked down.

"A Dark Soul," she whispered.

Dawn crouched with her. Her gaze darted back down the hall and then into the ICU. Leaning against the wall, Dawn asked, "Are you sure? I can't see anything."

Harley closed her eyes. "God, what's happening here?"

"We can't go in yet."

"What? That might be me in there coding. I have to go in."

Dawn scrubbed her hands together, clearly agitated. She had reason to be. Dark Souls were lurking nearby. Harley didn't know much about what was happening, but she'd seen enough to know that when they were around, someone died.

"Grab my hand." Harley stuck it out and then motioned to Dawn. "Come on. We don't have all day. Grab it."

Harley slapped Dawn's in hers and squeezed it. "Now beam us into my room."

"What? This isn't some sci-fi show, Harley."

"Get us in there, now," Harley said frantically.

A second later Harley was staring down at her lifeless body. A giant bandage covered the side of her head and eye. Tubing weaved in and out of her veins. Wires led to machines that silently beeped as her heart beat out a staccato tempo. There, draped over her body, was Renee, sobbing. On the other side of Harley's body, a doctor stood writing on a chart.

"Give me a break," Harley said, disgust lacing her voice. "Bitch couldn't care less about me."

"Why do you say that? Obviously she's distraught," Dawn said.

"It's all an act. I saw her cheating on me." Harley gave Dawn a puzzled look. "Don't you know what happened?"

Dawn shook her head.

"Hmm, well, I caught her cheating with one of my buddies. Former buddy," she said, walking over and touching Renee. As she picked up a lock of her hair, Harley wanted to yank it from her scalp. Instead, she tossed it over Renee's face. Startled, Renee sat back and looked at the doctor.

"What did you do that for?" Renee said, flipping her hair back.

"Do what?" He didn't even look up from his chart except to poke Harley, or at least Harley's body, with the tip of his pen. "This doesn't look good, my dear."

"But you said there was brain activity." Renee grabbed Harley's hand and pressed it to her face. "God, Harley, wake up. Please. For me."

"Like that's going to work." Harley walked to the other side of the bed. Peering down at herself, she touched her body. "This is not happening." She couldn't believe she was staring at her own corpse. "I think you owe me some answers." She turned, leaned against the bed rail, and searched Dawn's face. She was having a hard time accepting that she was lying in a bed yet also talking to Dawn, who wasn't exactly alive. "Am I in a coma?"

Dawn looked at Harley's body, at Renee, and

then back to Harley, who was standing in front of her. Her pensive look told Harley everything she needed to know.

Yep, she was near death.

Chapter Ten

"Did you hear her?" A Dark Soul popped into the room and appeared next to Harley.

A woman exploded in next to the man. "Yeah. I could've sworn the voice was coming from around here."

Harley had never seen a female…gatekeeper, was it?…so it shook her when the woman looked directly at her without seeing her. Pulling Dawn in, she whispered, "Shh, they can't hear me, but they can hear you, so don't say a word."

Hugging Dawn tight, Harley reached around and pulled her Beretta and aimed it at the woman's head.

In a flash, Dawn jerked the gun down.

What was she doing? Harley needed to dispatch these souls and find Jack. She surveyed them as they hovered over her body.

"When is this bitch going to die? I'm sick of waiting around."

"The boss says we stay, so we stay," the woman said, leaning against the wall and slipping through it.

"Ha, ha. You have to remember how to stabilize your energy, you dumb bitch," the man said, pulling her back into the room.

"Screw you. I haven't been doing this that long, so cut me some slack." She dusted herself off.

Why? Harley had no clue. It wasn't like they got dirty. Old habits die hard, Harley surmised.

"Who is she?"

The man walked around the bed and poked at Harley's body. "Got me, but she must be someone special, or the boss wouldn't have us sticking around to make sure she dies."

"Why don't you just help the process along?" the woman suggested. "It's not like anyone would know. She's going to die anyway, right?"

The man looked around as if considering the advice. Walking to the door, he looked down the hall and then glanced the other way. He was seriously considering the bitch's suggestion. What the fuck?

"He can't do that, can he?" Harley pulled back and asked Dawn.

"He's not—"

Harley slapped her hand over Dawn's mouth, but not before the woman ran toward them. Without thinking, Harley raised her gun and pressed it to the woman's head. As she pulled the trigger and the woman's head exploded like a firecracker-laced watermelon on the Fourth of July, she caught sight of the man's location. Without hesitating, she turned and aimed at him, and they locked eyes. Harley hesitated as a hint of recognition flashed across his face. It was the last time he'd see life on this side of the world. His path had been chosen for him. He was going to hell, where he belonged.

"Tell your boss I'm not going down without a fight."

He lunged sideways but was hit in the shoulder. Landing on his side, he grimaced in pain, then looked up and pointed at her.

"Can you still see me, you bastard?" Harley bent down and pressed the gun against his head.

"Fuck you. We'll get you like all the other Paladins. You won't live long."

Harley didn't say anything. Instead, she hit him with her gun, knocking him out. Why didn't she kill him? What was a Paladin? He was still a threat to Dawn, not her. She looked at Dawn, who hadn't moved.

"What does he mean, there are other Paladins?"

Dawn blanched at Harley's tone.

"What does he mean they'll get me like all of the others, Dawn?"

Dawn stepped away from Harley. She was putting herself in danger being so far away from Harley, but right now Harley didn't care. She wanted answers before she dispatched this bastard.

"Answer me." Harley stood and walked toward Dawn. Waving her gun in his direction, she demanded again, "What the hell is a Paladin? And explain how he can see me. They can see you, but not me. How?"

"How do you feel when you pull that trigger? When you are at the moment of deciding to kill them?"

"What do you mean?"

"How do you feel when you want to kill them?" Dawn asked again.

"I don't know. I guess I'm pissed that they want to kill you."

"At that very moment you're getting ready to pull the trigger, how do you feel?"

"I hate them. I hate what they do and I want to kill them," Harley finally admitted.

"That's when your soul is the darkest and you're the most vulnerable. They can see you at that moment. The longer you're in that state, the easier it is for them to kill you." Dawn put her hands on Harley's shoulders. "It's what gets a Protector killed."

"Oh, shit." That was all Harley could say. She'd never thought of why they could see her. She'd just assumed that it was an epiphany, a moment of utter clarity just before the death of their soul.

Harley walked over to the man and knelt beside him. Hate oozed from her. She wanted him dead, and she didn't care how it happened. If he woke now he would see her, see Dawn, and Harley couldn't have that, so she placed her hand on his chest. His heart vibrated under her touch. Black blood seeped between her fingers. It burned. She pushed her hand farther into his chest and instinctively wrapped her fingers around his heart. As she squeezed it, the man writhed in pain.

One last squeeze and he was dead.

His body burst into the black fog she'd come to recognize and he disappeared. He left nothing behind, not even dust. She still was amazed at the power that pulsed through her body. It was heady stuff, like when heroin was pushed through a vein. Closing her eyes, she relished the feeling, even though this could be dangerous if it continued.

A tang of remorse sliced through her. In this weird world she'd been thrown into, she'd taken a life. She had to do it to protect Dawn. Harley fell to her knees and cradled her head in her hands. A sob broke loose.

Dawn's warm touch flooded her body, replacing the sorrow she should have felt. Harley was engulfed in Dawn's embrace, which felt like a warm blanket. Dawn didn't feel like Jack; she wasn't cold. Warm breath caressed her neck as Dawn whispered in her ear.

"You had to do that, Harley. It's who you are, a Protector."

"A Protector?" Harley whispered. "Or a Paladin?"

Chapter Eleven

Harley startled as something smashed against the window. Furrowing her brows, she gazed at the window. She heard another crash against the outer wall, and something slammed against the window. As she raced to see what was going on, she tried to look down, but Dawn grabbed her arm and stopped her.

"What is it? What's happening?"

"Birds. Ravens, to be exact. They're the…" Dawn searched around the room and then ran to the door and peeked down the hall. "We need to go."

"What the hell?" Harley tried to peer out the window, but blood covered it. Moving to the next window, she looked down seven floors to the ground below. Birds writhed on the ground in some grotesque death dance. "What the fuck are those?"

"Harley!" Dawn yelled. Extending her hand, she trembled, waiting for Harley to grab it. "We need to go, now."

As soon as Harley touched Dawn, they morphed past two more Dark Souls reaching out in the direction of Dawn's voice, trying to grab her. Suddenly, Harley stood on a roof, clutching Dawn's hand in a death grip. They hadn't traveled far. The top of the hospital roof was recognizable. A giant landing circle was painted under their feet, and flashing landing lights throbbed their welcoming signal to an approaching helicopter.

"What the hell was that all about? What are those birds? They are birds, right?"

"They're the Dark Souls' watchers, their eyes, so to speak."

"I don't understand. Why were they hitting the window?"

"You killed their scions."

"Scions?" Harley didn't know the word, but she suspected it wasn't a good thing.

"Their implants, their splices. The Dark Souls are a part of the Ravens' lifeblood. The eyes of the birds see everything."

"And the Dark Souls can see through the birds." Harley's mind completed the thought before Dawn could confirm the craziness of what she'd just said. "This just gets weirder and weirder."

"When their offshoot is dying or has died, they kill themselves trying to get to them before they leave this plane."

"Christ."

Harley ran her hand through her hair, her fingers getting caught in the tangled mess of dried blood and curls, but something felt different. Gingerly, she explored around her scalp with her fingertips. The opening that had once been gaping was now closing. It was barely the size of a quarter.

"What's with my head?" Harley said, still poking around through her thick mane of hair.

"It's healing."

Throwing up her hands, she stopped Dawn. "Don't tell me. I don't want to know."

Was she or wasn't she dying?

The wind swirled around them, and the thump, thump, thump of an approaching helicopter kept

Harley from hearing Dawn's answer. It didn't matter. Nothing was normal in this world, and she didn't know why she was surprised by what she saw. She knew one thing, though. Below her feet, her body was in limbo.

"I need to get back down there," Harley cupped her mouth and yelled.

"What the heck are you two doing up here?" Jack shouted, standing at the sliding doors and dodging the gurney that was flying toward him. "Hey, watch where you're going with that thing."

Why he moved away when it would just go through him still surprised Harley. She guessed it took some time for people to get used to the fact that they didn't inhabit a real body, but merely the spirit of their body.

"Where the hell have you been?" Harley pulled him over to them. "Are you done pouting?"

"I wasn't pouting. I just needed some *me* time." He puffed out his chest and crossed his arms.

"Well, now that you're back, we can get the hell out of here and see about getting you to your gate," Harley screamed back at him.

"What?"

Before Harley could repeat her answer, a foul smell overtook them. Covering her nose with her shirt, she looked at Dawn and then Jack. He only shrugged and pulled his T-shirt up. Dawn's furrowed brows and her pursed lips worried Harley. Body language hadn't been her strong suit, but she knew enough to realize that this couldn't be good. Grabbing Dawn's hand and Jack's, she pulled them closer. Was her energy enough to keep them all shrouded from whatever was coming? God, she hoped so!

Hundreds of black birds started circling the

hospital, dropping feces that covered the roof. Pushing them under the overhang, Harley flattened against herself the wall, staring at the spectacle playing out around them.

"Word is out there's a new Protector," Dawn said softly. The sound of her voice would incite the rage of the birds, so she too flattened against the wall and grabbed Harley's hand. "How many have you killed?"

"What?" Harley peered out from under the awning.

"How many Dark Souls have you killed?"

Harley shrugged. She hadn't been keeping count. "Hell, I don't know—two, three, maybe."

"Think, Harley. How many have you killed since you've been on this side?"

"A few—five or six maybe." Harley counted out on her fingers. "You never answered my question back there. What's a Protector?"

"No shit? You're a Protector? Now that makes total sense. No wonder I was drawn to you. Damn." Jack slapped her on the back. "You're my Protector. Sweet!"

"Stop." She threw Jack's hand off her and turned to face Dawn. The screech of the birds wasn't helping her thought process. "Can you get us out of here?"

"Dude, just go through the doors. The damn birds can't follow you inside." Jack walked through the glass and waved. "See."

Simplicity was often lost on her. Shaking her head, she waved at the motion sensor and the door opened. She didn't have the luxury of morphing or walking through walls, but she could now appreciate those who did.

"We need to get as far away from here as possible.

The longer we're around here killing things, the more likely your body is going to attract attention. The Dark Souls can't kill you, they can't touch your body, but they can provoke you. I would imagine they're planning something to bring you out into the open so they *can* kill you. We've got to run, Harley."

Dawn made it a point to touch Harley when she talked to her. In return, Harley touched Dawn's face, studying it. Without thinking, Harley pulled Dawn in tight and landed a kiss. Her lips lingered on Dawn's. As she pushed her tongue against them, they parted and let her in. Her mind swam. Thoughts flowed like water rushing against an immovable barrier that had just broken loose. Renee, her job, riding her motorcycle, the exhilaration of fighting a fire. The adrenaline rush of breaking down a door and the flames that rolled up and kissed her when the backdraft hit. Her body flushed, her heart beat out of control, and all she wanted to do was sweep Dawn off her feet and take her somewhere more intimate.

The screeching caw of a bird pulled her out of the moment, reminding her of the danger they were all in.

"Damn!" Harley tried to catch her breath. Her body vibrated and her mind raced to keep up with all the sensations Dawn was throwing off. "Why are there so many birds? Are there that many Dark Souls around?" As when lightning strikes, the hair on her arms stood on end, and a shooting pain lanced through her heart.

"What the hell just happened?" She stopped and turned toward Dawn.

"You felt that?"

"Of course I felt that. It's like I've been hit by lightning."

"He's close." Dawn ran past Harley, grabbing her hand and pulling her down the stairwell. "We need to hurry."

"Who's close?" Harley asked.

Chapter Twelve

Harley jerked her arm back. She was tired, and it suddenly didn't matter who was chasing them. She couldn't move. Harley pulled Dawn into an embrace and kissed her again. She couldn't help it. Something came over her as she tried to wrestle with the idea she might die in the next ten or so minutes.

"Why did you do that? Harley, we need to go, now!" Dawn pulled back, still holding on to Harley's arms.

Harley had been fighting the urge to kiss Dawn again. She couldn't explain it, but she felt connected to Dawn. Love at first sight? Harley didn't believe in such nonsense, but she didn't have any other way of explaining the attraction she felt for Dawn. Perhaps being so close to dying induced some sort of pseudo-sexual response. All she knew was that Dawn was vexing.

"I can't explain what just happened. I've never done anything like that before. Sorry." Harley stepped back through the doors and walked a few steps so they would close. They left the evil outside, but her inner turmoil followed her inside. "I need to get something to eat and find a place to sleep." Harley ran down the stairs, pulling Dawn with her.

"Wow, way to hit on the angel, dude." Jack elbowed Harley as they walked down the stairs.

"Angel?"

"Yeah. You didn't know?"

"Fuck." Harley rolled her eyes. Yep, Captain Oblivious had replaced Captain Obvious. The signs were all there. The blue, warm light emanating off Dawn. The ease Harley felt around her. The way they could move throughout the world, or at least Harley's little part of the world. Dawn was quiet and unassuming. Harley was beguiled by her beauty, probably part of the mystique that went along with being an angel and getting people to do what they needed to do in times of trauma.

Shit!

"You're an angel?" Harley tossed over her shoulder as she hit the landing.

"I assumed you knew," Dawn said flatly, following her.

Every so often, Harley looked back over her shoulder. Dawn's face revealed a myriad of emotions, but fear had obviously taken hold of her at the moment. It surprised Harley. Weren't angels fearless? "We have to go."

They hit the crowded emergency room. Some were watching the burgeoning storm outside, and others milled about. Harley tried to push past people. What the hell was going on? She *had* to shove past people. Well, that was new. She felt people crowding her, brushing against her body. Moving someone off her, she noticed half his face was like raw meat, glass shards protruding from the mess.

"Jesus," she said, moving backward.

"Run. They're coming for you, my dear," he whispered, then moved her into the open twisting air.

The skies were like something out of a horror movie. Ravens flew around a backdrop of black clouds.

The air surrounding Harley and her group swirled. Trash, leaves, and debris kicked up around them. Dawn had stopped and was searching the sky.

"What are you looking for?" Harley yelled, shielding her face from the flying garbage that felt more like projectiles out to kill her. Pulling a few leaves from her mouth, she buttoned her shirt over her nose to protect her face. "Jesus, what the fuck is this shit?"

Dawn twirled in a circle, combing the black clouds for something. Harley followed Dawn's lead and started searching around too. "What are we looking for?"

"There." Dawn pointed toward a pinhole of light breaking through the clouds. It widened and cast a circle of light down somewhere miles in the distance. "We have to get there, Harley."

Harley started to run toward the light, but Dawn and Jack stopped her.

"You won't make it through this mess, Harley." Jack nodded at the circling birds.

The urge to run was never so present in Harley's mind. Fight or flight. Wasn't that what it was called? She didn't have enough bullets in her gun, and her knife would only do so much damage before they reached her. Assuming that's what the birds' intentions were. Hell, she didn't know what the fuck was happening, but she knew she needed to run like the devil.

"Then you get us the hell out of here." Harley stopped and crossed her arms, waiting for one of her companions to act.

Dawn and Jack looked at Harley and then swatted at the birds, who were starting to dive-bomb them. Claws scratched arms and drew blood. Once an animal caught the scent of blood, there would be a feeding frenzy. How did she know that?

"Well?"

"I'll take Harley, and you meet us at the light, Jack."

Poof, Jack was gone. Harley could have sworn she saw a Raven disappear with him, but she couldn't be sure. She still didn't know how all of this worked, so nothing would surprise her.

"We need to go, Dawn. I saw a Raven vanish with Jack. Can they do that?"

Fear replaced the calm that was always evident on Dawn's face. "We have to go. Hold on."

Harley was engulfed in feathers and blue light. Calmness enveloped her and she hugged Dawn tight. She couldn't help her body's response to touching Dawn, and she only hoped Dawn would forgive her *enlightened* state.

∿∿∿∿

"What the hell was that all about?" Harley asked, pulling leaves from her hair.

A huge spread of white wings protruded from Dawn's back. Wings? Suddenly they were withdrawn and were now hidden as if they had vanished. Wings? Where? Harley didn't have a clue. She did have to wonder why she wasn't protected when they morphed to this new location. Perhaps Dawn had launched Harley off her body when Harley started getting a sexual...it didn't matter. Picking herself up off the ground, Harley peered around the new surroundings. Her companions didn't look the worse for wear. She, on the other hand, was torn up.

"Where's the bird?" She was looking for the

Raven that had morphed with Jack.

When they didn't answer, Harley looked at them both. The two of them shared a look of distress, and then it passed.

"What?" Harley asked.

"He's gone. I assume he's on his way back to his Dark Soul. We need to get moving."

"Wait. Can someone just explain to me what the hell just happened back there at the hospital?"

Dawn and Jack shared another look. Jack pointed to Dawn and said, "You tell her."

"Tell me what?"

"They say one comes every century."

"One what?" She was losing her patience with the ambiguity circle crap they were talking in, so she asked again. "What century thing?"

"It's you, Harley. You're the Paladin."

"Paladin. What does that mean?"

More questions, but no answers. She'd had enough. "You know what? I'm going to the hospital. I've had enough of this nonsense, this talking in riddles. I'm crawling back into my body and ending this bullshit."

"You can't." Jack grabbed her arm, stopping her.

Harley looked down at his hand and then back at his face. "You better remove that, or there's going to be hell to pay right here, buddy."

"Harley, please reconsider. Jack needs to get to his gate. Someone out there doesn't want him to make it. You're his Paladin. You've got to help him."

"I'm not anything. I'm just Harley, and I'm going to wake up from this bad nightmare and chalk it up to the head injury I suffered." Harley reached up and touched where the injury should have been. It was gone.

A few matted hairs were the only thing reminiscent of the hole that had only hours ago been gaping open.

"Take your shirt off," Dawn ordered her.

"Excuse me? You get pissed because I kiss you, and now you want me to take my shirt off? What kind of crazy are you?" Harley pushed away from the two standing before her.

"Do you have a birthmark on your chest?"

Harley reached up and covered her right breast. How could Dawn know about the wine stain?

"No."

"Prove it," Dawn demanded.

Harley hesitated and then pulled her shirt down off her shoulder. A tattoo hid the birthmark. Before Harley could say anything, Dawn touched the tattoo and the birthmark reappeared.

Harley jerked back. "How did you do that?"

"You can't hide who you are, Harley. You've had this for centuries."

Harley stood paralyzed, trying to decipher Dawn's cryptic words.

Jack screamed, grabbing her attention. "Harley, you have to help me get to my gate, or I'll be stuck here." His eyes darted back and forth looking for something, probably the Raven. She watched as he started to hyperventilate.

Dropping to his knees, he cradled his face in his hands and started to wail again. "Oh, God, what am I going to do?"

Dawn wrapped her arms around him to offer comfort, but he was beyond consoling.

"I'm going to be one of those lost souls. I'm going to be stuck here. Oh, Christ."

Jack rocked back and forth. He wrung his hands,

and tears etched a path down his face. He buried his face in Dawn's shoulder.

"What's he talking about?" Harley asked. Agitated, she nervously walked a circle around the two kneeling on the ground. She didn't know why she did it, but her pacing relaxed the group.

"If a Paladin dies, the people they were sent to guide to the gate are destined to stay in this plane. They can't move forward or to the next level. They'll never be reborn. They'll be stuck here to wander aimlessly." Dawn spread her hands wide. "Unless another Paladin offers to take them to their gate."

"Look, I'm not some priest. I can't exorcise some demon out and help them move on."

"That's Catholic doctrine, Harley. This is something much higher than some church teachings. This is a basic, natural order. We go back to the beginning of life."

"I have no idea what you're talking about."

Harley continued to pace around the two of them. Her mind raced as she worked on what Dawn had said. A calm came over her and she stopped. As she looked up to the peaceful skies for answers, something in her subconscious told her the fact she was the new Paladin was right. She knew it, she felt it; it was like something in her bones told her. Before she was even an event between her mother and father, this role was preordained for her.

"You know," a voice in her head answered.

Harley twirled around and searched for whoever had spoken. "Who said that?"

Harley looked down at Dawn. Again, Harley sucked at reading body language, but all the signs pointed to Dawn. "You?" Harley asked without speaking aloud.

Dawn only nodded, then went back to comforting Jack. She cradled his head and hummed some melodious tune.

Harley's mind raced, tumbled.

"Take your birthmark," Dawn said. "How long have you known about its origins?"

"I've dreamt about this godforsaken thing since I was a child." Harley closed her eyes, squeezing them tight.

"Are you sure they were dreams?" Dawn asked, touching Harley's shoulder.

Thinking harder, Harley caught bits and pieces, fragments of memories with her nana. Popping her eyes open, she searched Dawn's face for answers. What did Dawn know? Why was she so persistent? Of course Harley had dreamt of the mark. Vivid, glorious, colorful dreams. Sometimes, they were so real she felt like she'd touched everything, smelt the flowers, and lived a hundred lives and died a thousand times. She suddenly felt like she'd been sucking on cotton as her mouth dried. Her tongue swollen, she smacked her mouth, trying to speak. Words weren't the only things escaping her at the moment. Then she remembered.

It was a hot, sweltering summer day in southern Alabama. Her annual visit to her grandmother's small, quaint trailer that was more like a smoker than a home. Nights were bearable only when the swamp cooler was working in her grandmother's bedroom. Pretty soon, her aunts, uncles, and cousins would be there, and her time with her grandmother's home would turn into a circus. The only thing missing were the animals. How her nana handled all that activity was beyond her. Harley was wiped out after swimming, playing endless games of hide- and-seek, and fishing. She loved to fish.

One day some of the kids at the local swimming pool in her grandmother's trailer park had teased and tormented her, and her nana had pulled Harley onto her lap, rocked her, and explained something she would never forget.

Harley looked back at Dawn. "No, I learned about the mark from my nana. She spoke of great warriors whose job was to lead souls to Valhalla."

She remembered her nana's finger tracing the mark as she explained its meaning.

"Only the strong were given this mark, honey. It is passed to one who was deemed worthy to lead." Nana grasped Harley's face between her bony fingers and meaty palm and kissed her.

"Naw-uh," Harley said, blushing at the kiss.

Nana pulled back in mock surprise. "Do you not believe me, Granddaughter?"

Harley's whole body shook as her grandmother tickled her. Nana looked around, pulled the tissue from her bra strap, and showed Harley her own markings. Nana's were more elaborate and beautiful, but similar to Harley's.

Casting her gaze from the birthmark to her nana, Harley sobered.

"You, my child, are the chosen one. Odin chose no such warrior women. Only Mother built the tribe of Protectors. For Odin, all souls who died in battle went to Valhalla and didn't need his protection. All others didn't deserve his attention. So they were destined to wander, prey for all the evil that wandered the place

between Valhalla and Purgatory: The Gatekeepers, former Protectors who moved into the darkness for power."

"Why?"

"Mother wanted to save and protect those souls so they could reach their next life or the heavens. She created the Paladins as the answer. Unfortunately, as with any system of justice or protection, there are those who decide that they want more power. The darkness attracts them—

the   power,   the   corruption—hence,   The Gatekeepers."

"Do my mom and dad have this?" Harley rubbed her T-shirt over her birthmark.

"No. The Paladin is chosen, their future seen before they are born. You must have something great in your future, child."

"Like what?" Harley didn't understand what her grandmother was saying.

She wouldn't for years, but that conversation, as others, would play over and over in her head. Especially after the dreams started.

Chapter Thirteen

Ｈow did all of this happen?" Harley sat across from Dawn and Jack. Hugging her knees, she rocked back and forth. Nothing was making any sense.

Centuries.

Angels.

Wings.

Ravens.

Paladin.

Nothing was seeping to the top of this quagmire of unrealistic expectations. Harley was trying to wrap her brain around what Dawn was telling her. Wouldn't she know if she was a Paladin? Hell, didn't people who had past lives feel it? Did they have some inclination that they'd been here before? She didn't. She was just Harley—a volunteer firefighter and schoolteacher, born to Madeline and Fritz. Her first kiss was with a girl in the boathouse when she was eight. That she remembered, but a past life? Hell no. She was lucky if she remembered the dream from the night before.

Dawn's soothing voice pulled Harley back to reality. "That shooting back at the campground wasn't an accident. You were targeted, Harley."

"What?" Harley reflectively touched her head again, running her fingers through her scalp. This was playing out more like a bad dream than anything real. Nothing, no blood, no opening in her head, nothing. It was all gone, like it had never been there. "Why now? Jesus, I'm thirty-eight years old. Isn't that a little late in life to become a Paladin?"

Dawn shrugged. "You weren't ready." Dawn stood, grabbed Harley's hands, and held them tight. "You opened a channel that night, or maybe a Dark Soul was sent to convince you that taking your own life was the only way out of your misery. I'm not sure. You won't age like everyone else, Harley. Time has a way of bending for a Paladin."

"Okay, but back to that Dark Soul convincing me to kill myself. They can do that?"

"Not normally. There are rules, but lately it seems things are out of balance. When someone does something like that, they're waiting. If a Dark Soul is lucky and the person takes their life, a Dark Soul is there ready to kill their soul."

"So they're like vultures waiting for the carcass to die before they feed on them." Realization was verging on clarity for Harley.

"They strike when someone is at their weakest."

"But Jack." Harley pointed at him, still rocking back and forth. He was almost catatonic.

"He wasn't weak, he was drunk. There's a difference."

"You mean there is honor among this group of killers?" Harley almost laughed.

"No, there are rules. If they break the rules, they forfeit their life. Simple as that. Unfortunately, I don't think they knew you were a Paladin," Dawn said.

Harley still wasn't sure she understood, but she was trying. "And me..." She pointed her thumbs into her chest. "I was weak? No fucking way."

"Think about it. You had two bullets in your

hand. Remember?"

She did.

Mentally clicking off another day, she sat staring at the two bullets in her other hand. Picking up the fine-point Sharpie she'd been writing in her journal with, she scribbled I'm done on one and Fuck this on the other. She was too much of a coward for suicide, but she had considered it lately, a lot. Sitting at night in her tent, she could feel the cold steel bump of the 9mm she had tucked under her pillow for protection. Now it lay cradled in her lap, the clip pulled out and the bullets scattered around her. She'd even formulated a half-assed plan one night while lying in her sleeping bag.

She could wrap herself in her plastic liner and not make a mess someone else would have to clean up. She'd seal it with duct tape and get inside her sleeping bag, which was in her tent that she would collapse around her for more protection. Then she'd take out her cook pot, place it over her head, and put the gun in her mouth. But which way should she aim the gun? Straight back at her spinal cord or at an angle into her brain? By putting the cook pot over her head, she was certain the bullet wouldn't travel and hurt anyone. She didn't want to be careless with someone else's life.

"But I didn't."

"No, but those guys camping down the way from you..."

"Yeah."

"They did."

During a lousy night of tossing and turning, she'd dreamt of her lover and watching her over and over again kissing that bitch she'd spied her with. She got up, took a piss, and walked the campgrounds. It was too hot for campers, except a few die-hard guys who stayed at the opposite end of the grounds. From the looks of their camp, they were there to hunt and party, if the empty whiskey bottles and beer cans lying around were any indication. Stepping backward, she retreated the way she'd come and put as much distance between her and them as she could. No use inviting trouble, even if it did seem to have a way of finding her.

"Shit. I remember them laughing it up and partying all through the night. I didn't think I would ever get to sleep if it wasn't for a little nightcap."

"Dark Souls have power. Remember that doctor back at the hospital? Remember the dark aura around him?"

"Shit." Harley had vaguely seen it, but she'd been too caught up in Renee to give it another thought.

"But he wasn't one of them."

"No, but if the soul is willing, if there's something inside already black, they can push until the person is no longer in control."

"This isn't happening." Harley grasped her head, closed her eyes, and started humming to herself. Rocking back and forth, she knew if she just wished hard enough, she'd wake up from this nightmare and be back in the hospital. While that didn't sound great, it was a whole lot better than being stuck in some bullshit dream. What was she going to do now? Jack's future was firmly resting on her shoulders, and she hated the added pressure. If she did nothing, he was stuck here in limbo, but if she accepted what Dawn was saying, if she was a Paladin, what did *her* future hold?

Chapter Fourteen

Every hour seemed to bring more questions than answers. Harley could go back and hopefully reenter her body, or she could accept that she was what Dawn called her: a Paladin. Either way her life would never be the same. Harley looked around, trying to get her bearings.

"Where are we, and what was that light all about?" She didn't direct her question to anyone in particular, but clearly Jack, who was still sobbing, wasn't in any condition to answer her. She doubted he knew anything anyway. So, that left Dawn. What was it about Dawn that made her come unglued? Was it the whole angel thing? That was definitely throwing her for a loop. Harley couldn't deny she felt a connection to Dawn. Then there was the whole mind-meld thingy they had going on. Yep, she was definitely screwed no matter what she decided.

"Anyone, Earth to Bueller." Harley snapped her fingers.

Dawn piped up. "You know that thing about light at the end of the tunnel? Well, light can guide us. The Dark Souls obviously have the darkness. The universe sends us a light to bring us out of a bad situation."

"Sounds a little clichéd, don't you think? I mean the good guys wear white and the bad guys…well, you get my drift."

Harley couldn't sit still. Her nerves were frayed,

and adrenaline was rushing through her like speed. It kept her alert and moving. After the calamity she'd just witnessed, she'd just as soon keep her guard up.

"So why doesn't the universe," Harley said, making air quotes, "just show guys like Jack where their gate is?"

"It doesn't work like that. There's a balance, at least there's supposed to be, and right now it's off kilter. I can't explain it." Dawn stood and spread her hands wide. "All of this—

nature, animals, people—there's an order to things, and lately someone has stuck their hand in the middle of it and stirred it up. All I know, all any of us know, is that someone wants everything for themselves, and they don't want souls getting to the other side."

"But why?" Harley wasn't convinced that Dawn knew what the hell was going on.

"A soul gets reborn and a new life begins, again. If you stop that, then there are more Dark Souls and they make an army and an army does what?"

Harley shrugged. She couldn't buy a vowel with the little she knew, so she didn't have a clue where all this was going.

Dawn provided an answer. "They conquer."

"Oh."

"Are your mom and dad alive, Harley?"

"Sure, but you knew that already."

"You've seen what you've seen in just a day or so. Do you want them to have someone to guide them and protect them to their gate?"

Harley stopped pacing. "Are you saying—"

"Stop. They're fine. It was a rhetorical question. I'm trying to get you to understand the gravity of the situation and realize how important you are, what role you play in the bigger picture."

"I didn't ask for this," Harley reminded Dawn. Stubbing her foot into the dirt, she added, "Besides, I was never a big-picture kinda gal. More of a microcosm one."

"Well, right now you're the chosen."

"Well, unchoose me, so I can go back to my life. So I can wake up and get—"

"Back to Renee?"

"It's my life, right?"

Harley's stomach grumbled. Her body was letting her know that the high she was on was starting to dissipate. The hair on the back of her neck was standing up again, and the setting sun meant only one thing. Things go bump in the night. She could only wonder what happened when the world went black.

"I need to sleep. Do you sleep or eat? No, I don't suppose you do, do you?"

"I can." That was all Dawn offered.

"Well, I've got to clear my head and think about all this, but my body is running out of juice."

"You're still going to have to pay attention to your body, Harley. You won't survive here or back there on adrenaline alone." Dawn pulled Jack to his feet. "Come on. We need to find somewhere safe."

"Wait, as long as you're with me, they can't see you...right?"

"We all need to be touching you or within your... aura. Then they can't see us, but they can still smell a larger group of us and hear us, remember?"

So much had happened, Harley wouldn't have remembered her own name if Dawn hadn't repeated it a hundred times today. "Does this job come with a rule book or something?"

"It'll come with time," Dawn said, pulling Jack along.

Harley figured she'd learn it the hard way, like every other lesson in her life. "Can we at least find some place to crash for the night?"

"Where do you think we're going, Captain Obvious?" Dawn said, pulling Jack along.

Harley ignored the snipe. "Let me help you with him. Come on, you big baby."

Harley grabbed Jack's arm and wrapped it around her shoulders. She didn't want him dying on her watch. Harley stopped. What the hell was she saying? The guy was already dead. The gaping hole in his chest was a bloody reminder that she wasn't in Kansas, or wherever she'd started off from last night. Maybe getting some sleep was what she needed. Waking up held promise that it would all be an awful nightmare.

"Are you going to save me, Harley?"

"We'll talk in the morning, Jack. Assuming you're here when I wake up."

Harley hoped he wasn't, but with the way her luck was going, there was no telling what she would find when she awoke. Searching for a safe place was proving to be more difficult than Harley expected. The dense woods offered a little protection, but only at a surface level. If one of them turned over and away from her, they risked being discovered, and she wasn't too sure of her ability to protect them at the moment. Her body rebelled against Jack's weight on her shoulders, and her energy was just about sapped.

"How long have we been walking?"

"I don't know. An hour maybe."

"Next time, can you put us somewhere closer to a mall, a hotel, or a fried-chicken place?"

"I'll take that under advisement when we're running for our lives again. Which, at the rate we're going, should be any minute," Dawn snapped again.

So she does have human emotions. Good to know. Harley mumbled, "I'm just sayin'."

"Do you see that?" Dawn pointed off to the left.

Harley squinted but couldn't make anything out. "Nope, I left my X-ray glasses back at the campground. Wait, I think I have them in my backpack." She made a show of shifting the pack.

"Stop it, Harley. I know you're tired. We're all spent."

"Sorry." She pushed herself forward, practically harnessing all of Jack's weight on her shoulders. "Why were you at that pond yesterday? You were a sitting duck out in the open. A Dark Soul could have taken you."

"They can't hurt me. Besides, I was waiting for you."

"Me?" Harley looked around Jack, trying to see Dawn. A pang of familiarity struck her again.

"I'm not as easy to kill as they think." Dawn pulled Jack over onto her shoulders.

"Hmm." Harley didn't know what that meant, but she was tired of talking in riddles. "Can I get a straight answer from you, please?"

"I think I see that light again. Look, right there. See it?"

☙ ❧ ☙ ❧ ☙

Like scenes from a silent movie, short bursts of thoughts played out the events from earlier in the day in Harley's brain. Did she actually put her hands inside a man's chest and squeeze his heart, killing him?

"Great, now I have insomnia to boot," she whispered. Staring off into the darkness, she tried to sleep, but everything was jumbled in her head. Birds, Dark Souls, Renee throwing herself over her body in such a dramatic fashion, and Dawn. All images that her overactive imagination kept on a repeat loop. She was having a hard time reconciling the fact that she'd gone from saving lives in her job as a firefighter to teaching young souls—who might turn out to be Dark Souls in the future—to taking lives in her new life as a Paladin.

Five.

She'd killed five people today. *Well, they weren't really people, but sorta people-like.* Maybe looking at the Dark Souls as something out of a horror movie would help her justify what she'd done? They weren't exactly living, breathing humans, were they? So many questions and not enough answers. Her brain was fried. Now, if she could just do a hard shutdown and reboot in the morning. Her usual off switch, a shot of bourbon, was nowhere to be had, so she lay there suffering in silence. Her stomach grumbled. Clearly, food was still important; at least she felt hungry. How was she going to survive on this plane?

The drone of crickets and the rustle of leaves as the wind cut through the trees meant she was still alive, right? Out of the corner of her eye, she spied Jack lying on his back, his hands on his chest rising up and down as he took long, deep breaths. The sleep of the dead, isn't that what they called it when her dad couldn't be roused? Funny how that was actually something in this world.

Her thoughts turned to Dawn. What was she

to make of Dawn? She was so soft spoken, yet she had the strength of ten men. The way she threw one of her attackers against the wall at the hospital was intimidating. Yet she didn't kill him. Why? Harley had been the one to do that. Holding up her hand, she clenched it, then held it open, examining it as if it was foreign to her. Without thinking, she'd shot them. Killed the Dark Souls without a second thought. It was as if she knew she had to do it. A hint of remorse and then they were gone. Nothing left behind but a dense black fog that felt more like a sunburn when it touched the skin.

Was she a Paladin? She didn't feel special. She didn't have special powers in this world, just her guts, a gun, and a knife. Harley caressed the gun in her waistband. She'd need more bullets. She had only one clip in her backpack. She was a killing machine, and killing machines needed to stay primed and ready for action. The way she was dispatching Dark Souls, the last clip she had wouldn't last the day, and if they didn't find Jack's gate soon…well, she didn't want to think about what might happen to them if she didn't get Jack to his destination.

Pulling her knife out of her pocket, she flicked it open and spun it between her fingers. This would mean she had to get up close and personal with the Souls. She remembered how easy it had been to reach into a man's chest and squeeze the life out of him. She'd looked into his eyes and seen the hateful rage he regarded her with. If she hadn't killed him, he would have definitely killed her in that split second he could see her. It was the only time she was vulnerable, so she'd have to be careful. Folding the knife, she slipped it back into her pocket. It was her last resort. She studied her hands. No, these were her last resort. They would never fail her.

Harley thought about what Dawn had said about her mom and dad. Would she want someone to be there for them? To guide them to the other side, to protect them as they went to their gate? Of course. Perhaps it would be her. Was that allowed? Were there rules against a Paladin protecting family members? She doubted it. This wasn't the kind of work where you couldn't be hired if a family member worked for the county. This was higher than that. Isn't that what Dawn had said?

Harley worried about her parents, about their guide. If there wasn't someone waiting for them, they would be stuck, wandering, evading, and trying to stay alive like Jack. Like the man at the hospital who had pushed her out into the storm. He looked like a mangled mess. Guess she should get used to seeing people broken up like that. Was he waiting for his guide? So many questions that she couldn't seem to comprehend what was real, what was a dream, and what lived on this plane of existence. Nothing made sense anymore.

A flutter at the barn door pulled at her attention. Snatching her gun from her pants, she aimed it at the door and waited. It opened slowly, just wide enough for someone to step through. Harley caught a glimpse of wings and relaxed as Dawn struggled to get herself, wings and all, through the opening. She watched as Dawn tucked the delicate span somewhere behind her. She'd have to ask Dawn how she hid all that feather and wing and managed to look so human.

Angel.

Whatever!

"You awake?" Dawn whispered, sitting next to her.

"Yeah. Couldn't sleep."

"You need to get some rest. If today is anything like yesterday, well…" Dawn tossed an apple on Harley's stomach and then another.

"How do you do that? Tuck your wings in?"

Dawn bit her lip and looked past Harley at Jack.

Harley pressed on. "I feel like we've met before."

Still Dawn didn't say anything, not even a hint that she heard Harley.

Harley was realizing just how good Dawn was at avoiding things she didn't want to talk about, but Harley was persistent. Dawn would find that out, eventually.

Rubbing an apple on her pant leg, she asked, "Where'd you get these?"

"Out back. You're going to need something a little more substantial. When it's light out, we'll see what the owners have in store for breakfast."

"I'm not sure about any of this…" Harley pointed to their surroundings and finally at Jack. She took a bite of the apple.

"I know," Dawn said, touching Harley's knee. A warm feeling sped through Harley. If she didn't know better she would say they were sharing a moment. "I'm confident you'll make the right decision, for you." Dawn smiled and then lay on her side facing Harley.

"So, if I decide to help Jack, what's the plan?"

"You get him to his gate."

"How?"

"It'll come to you, Harley. I'm just here for you. To protect you."

"Like back at the hospital?"

"Like back at the hospital."

"Why can't you take Jack to his gate?"

"It doesn't work like that. I'm only here for you."

Harley nodded like she understood, when in reality, she still didn't have a clue what Dawn meant. "So there are layers of bureaucracy here, too?" Harley laughed. "Gotta love it. Is there a big guy, or gal, you work for?"

"Sorta."

"Sorta, great. You've got the vagueness thing down pat. So how about some answers, and don't tell me that all-will-be-revealed-in-due-time bullshit." Harley could sense Dawn was struggling internally, judging by the way she bit her lip, then pursed her lips and avoided looking at Harley. Slowly, her soft oval face relaxed. Her lips barely parted, and she took a long, deep breath. If she was trying to seduce Harley, it was too late. Harley was on a slow burn for Dawn already. Looking closer, Harley realized Dawn had fallen asleep.

Great, she thought, tossing the apple core off into the barn. Pushing some hay together, she lay on her back and threaded her fingers behind her head. She followed the beams of moonlight pushing through the splits in the barn timbers. Home was somewhere distant, probably a memory for now. Would she ever see her mom and dad again or get out of that coma and have a normal life? Maybe she could help get Jack to his gate, and then it would all be over. That's what she would do. She'd get Jack to the other side, and then she'd part ways with Dawn, slip back into her own skin, and live a new life. She would take whatever it offered her and run.

❧ ❧ ❧ ❧

"Harley, honey, can you help me? An old woman reached out toward Harley. Her gnarled fingers stretched to touch Harley, but she stepped back, out of reach.

"Mom?" The voice sounded familiar, shaky but familiar.

"Oh, don't tell me you don't recognize your own mother?"

The woman latched onto Harley's arm and pulled her closer. Perfume wafted around them, a scent Harley had smelled a hundred times. Her mother's perfume.

"We've got to go find your father. I'm afraid he's wandered off again."

Without thinking about how bizarre all of this was, Harley went along. "Why would Dad wander off?"

"Well, ever since the accident, he's been a different man. He's taken it upon himself to find our gate."

"Gate? Accident? What accident, Mom?"

"Oh, Harley, honey. You remember. We were driving home from the cabin the other night. Your father…" The woman patted Harley's arm just like her own mom always did when she was explaining something and she wanted Harley to pay attention. "It was late and I wanted to wait until morning, but he was in such a hurry to get home. Said he was missing Ms. Kitty."

Ms. Kitty was the new kitten her parents had just rescued. Her dad wasn't a cat person, so it shocked Harley when he'd brought it out cuddled up on his arm at her last visit.

"Anyway, that big ol' semi just was a shifting and swaying back and forth. I think the poor driver fell asleep at the wheel. Next thing you know it spilled its *load right in front of your father."*

Harley sucked in a breath, shocked at what she was hearing. Cupping the woman's face, Harley studied her eyes. They were the same blue as her mother's, only a little lighter from age.

"Honey, are you all right?"

"I'm...I'm fine." Harley let a smile cross her face before she kissed her mom's forehead.

"Well, if you're done with this stare-down, help me find your father." Madeline pulled Harley's hand from her face and jerked Harley's arm. Suddenly, following her mom, Harley felt four years old again.

A speeding car almost hit Harley as she walked down the side of the highway. "Asshole."

"Harley Jean."

Yep, it was her mom.

"Sorry." It was funny how even in a dream, Harley reverted back to her younger self. Her mom was someone you didn't mess with, but she was also the kindest, most tender-hearted person Harley knew.

In the passing headlights of the car, Harley could see two people wrestling.

"Hey," Harley yelled. She recognized the man on the left as her father, or at least an older version of him, but the other guy was a—

"Mom!" Harley clutched her throat. She couldn't breathe. Her body went rigid, as if she was paralyzed with fear. Her heart was racing so fast she thought she might be having a heart attack. She had no control over her body and was panicking.

"Harley, Harley, look at me." Dawn loomed over her, but Harley could barely see her. Harley tried to relax. "It's okay." Dawn turned Harley's face and placed a kiss on her lips. Instantly, Harley's muscles felt like they were melting. Sucking in a deep breath, she sat up and gulped in air.

"What the fuck? What just happened? I saw my mom and dad, at least that's who I think they were. They were so old that I didn't recognize my mom. She touched me." Harley rambled on quickly, then touched the exact place her mother had moments earlier. "She called me by name, and I could smell her perfume. She said they'd been in an accident and that my dad had wandered off and…" Harley sucked in another breath.

"It was a dream, Harley. Just a dream."

Chapter Fifteen

A dream. It felt so real, so…" Harley scrubbed her face. She'd seen the Dark Soul wrestling her father to the ground. He'd raised his hand and plunged it into her father's chest. Where was his Protector? Why was her mother wandering around a busy highway? Just a dream, Dawn said. More like a nightmare.

"My parents. They were…" Harley choked up. She tried to talk around the lump in her throat, but she couldn't.

She began to sob uncontrollably, and suddenly she felt herself sheathed in warmth as Dawn wrapped herself around her. Harley wasn't one for flagrant displays of emotion, like crying, but she couldn't help herself. She tried to push Dawn off, but the stress of the day had taken its toll, and all she could do was embrace the release.

"Your parents are fine, Harley. Trust me."

"I just saw them the other day. My dad got a cat. He doesn't even like cats," Harley said, not knowing why she was sharing something so trivial with Dawn. Dawn didn't care about her parents.

"They're okay, Harley."

"My parents are all I have." Harley wished she could call her mom. She was Harley's lifeline in the Renee world of crap. They'd spent more than a few nights talking late. Angie never complained, never spoke ill of Renee. She only encouraged Harley to do what she thought was right. God, how she would love to talk to her mom right now.

"They're going to live a long and wonderful life. You just need to focus on you right now," Dawn said, trying to comfort Harley.

Harley leaned back and looked at Dawn. "Will I ever see them again?"

"Probably." That was all Dawn offered.

Harley watched Dawn's lips part. A moment passed, and then Dawn lowered her head and kissed Harley. Her mind fired as her body responded to Dawn's soft response. She touched Dawn in a way that felt familiar, like they'd done this dance a thousand times before. It was the caress of lovers who knew each other's body, bodies that had shared a lifetime of love. Without thinking, she ran her hand along Dawn's hip and then to her breast. Dawn didn't resist. In fact, she felt compliant under Harley's touch. Suddenly embarrassed by her forwardness, Harley slid her hand down the curve of Dawn's waist and rested it on her hip. Everything felt so familiar

As Dawn touched Harley's chest, the tattoo suddenly felt warm under Dawn's hand. She pulled her head back and studied Harley's face. Her smile widened, and Harley felt like she was under some heavenly spell. Dawn's eyes were like fathomless pools with stars in them. The blue light that always surrounded Dawn was now almost…purple. It was so surreal, Harley wasn't sure she could ever explain what she was seeing. She was cognizant of only Dawn. Her body felt like it was floating on a whisper of air, with nothing below her and only Dawn above her, their bodies barely touching. Yet it was like they were electrically charged, the sexual energy igniting the air around them.

Harley reached out and pulled Dawn to her. She slipped her hand under Dawn's sweater and caressed the silky-smooth skin of her taut stomach. Dawn pulled Harley's hips against her own. Sliding her hands into Harley's jeans, she parted her legs and Harley slipped a thigh between them. Dawn gasped at the contact. Her neck arched, and she panted as Harley slid completely between her legs.

"What's happening?" Harley whispered into Dawn's ear before she bit the lobe next to her lips.

"Harley?"

"Yeah," she grunted out. She wasn't sure she could speak more than a few words, her mind swimming.

"I…I don't think we should…" Dawn rasped, her body responding to Harley's touch.

Harley lifted her off of her feet as she pulled them both to standing and commanded, "Wrap your legs around my waist."

Every nerve in Harley's body was firing. She'd been on an adrenaline rush from the moment she met Jack. She loved the adrenaline her job provided, was a junkie. After fighting a fire all night all she wanted to do when she got home was burn off the residual energy, and a hard workout or quick fuck with Renee was always good at helping her light her own fire. While their relationship lacked any spark, the same couldn't be said about their love life. That was the only thing that didn't suck.

"Harley," Dawn gasped as Harley palmed her ass.

Harley carried them deeper into the barn away from Jack. Spying a few hay bales stacked in a pile, Harley gently set Dawn on them. They were the perfect height as Harley let her lips explore Dawn's. Traveling down the silky neck before her, Harley stopped at the throbbing pulse. Her own raced as she took her time exploring Dawn. She reached up Dawn's back, caressing the slender, taut muscles. Her fingertips traveled farther up Dawn's spine, and Harley felt her shudder and then release a soft moan that only further kindled Harley's lust. Moving her lips farther down, she licked Dawn's collarbone, then let her tongue travel to Dawn's shoulder as she unbuttoned her blouse. Harley dropped to her knees as she pushed the fabric out of her way, kissing each breast through the lace cups of Dawn's bra. Dawn's nipples hardened. God, she could devour Dawn here and now. What was stopping her?

Dawn pulled Harley's head against her chest and held it firmly. Her heart battled with her head, and she knew Dawn could feel it. Harley pulled Dawn's hand toward her and kissed her palm, then rubbed it against her cheek. She wanted Dawn in a way she couldn't explain. There was something about Dawn. Something she felt—no, knew. They had shared moments like this in the distant past. She didn't want to think about that now. She wanted release, and Dawn was the only one who could provide her with that. Pulling Dawn's hips closer, she dipped her head and nuzzled Dawn's stomach. Each kiss made Dawn squirm.

"Ticklish?"

"A little," Dawn huffed out.

Stoic, Harley said with some reservation, "This may be the last time for me, Dawn."

"It won't be." Dawn sounded resolute in her declaration.

Harley looked up at Dawn, searching for something. All she saw was love reflected back at her.

"Don't tell me you know my future, too."

Dawn cradled Harley's face in her hands, smiled, and then kissed Harley with an abandon Harley had never felt before. She pulled Harley to her feet, yanked at the button-down shirt still tucked into Harley's jeans, and pulled Harley on top of her.

Harley giggled like a schoolgirl. She felt like a nervous teenager who'd snuck out of her parents' home and was breaking all the rules.

"What's so funny?" Dawn asked around her kisses.

"I laugh when I'm nervous. I was just thinking how I felt like a teenager and here we are in a barn sneaking around."

"I make you nervous?" Dawn smiled.

"You make me…" Harley stopped and thought about what it was about Dawn that made her so… perhaps nervous wasn't the right word. Intrepid. Somewhere deep down inside her soul, she wanted to protect Dawn. Harley felt fearless, heroic, and gallant when she was around Dawn.

Harley pushed the thoughts out of her mind away, pulled Dawn's shirt off, and then stopped. "God, you're beautiful."

Dawn's aura had changed to a sizzling fuchsia.

"Is this what happens when you're turned on?"

"You should see me when I'm mad." Dawn's tongue darted out and flicked against Harley's lips.

Christ. I'm going to lose my mind, you're so fucking hot!

No, you won't. But if you don't finish what you've started, I'm going to lose mine.

Dawn was whispering through her head. As Dawn looking down at Harley, her smoldering expression almost brought Harley to her proverbial knees. They were at that level again. Nothing said verbally, their minds connecting on a different plane.

Don't think about it, just react. Dawn pulled Harley back into her embrace.

"Won't you get in trouble for this?" Harley said out loud.

Dawn flipped Harley onto her back and shook her hair, covering Harley's face and offering some privacy between them.

"Don't overthink this, Harley, or we'll lose our moment. We don't know what tomorrow will bring us."

"Now you're sounding like me."

Harley pulled Dawn down into a tight embrace, laced her fingers into Dawn's hair, and tortured Dawn's lips with her own. Dawn's skin felt like it was on fire. Each kiss smoldered as Harley laid a path of passion down Dawn's body, starting at her breasts and stopping at the top of Dawn's jeans. She hesitated, fumbling with the button. She wasn't as polished as she thought she was, so Dawn offered helped. Something slipped between them, merging them together. Harley felt her life suddenly entwine with Dawn's. The pull was so strong it scared Harley.

Heart and mind raced in opposite directions. One on a primal course, the other...well, Harley could only describe it as a more spiritual one, yet both parts of her wanted the same thing: Dawn.

"Here, let me," Dawn said impatiently.

"I'm sorry. I'm not usually this—"

Dawn put a finger to Harley's lips, smiled, then kissed her again. *It's all right. It's been a while for me, too.*

With a flourish, Dawn's wings fluttered wide and

wrapped around them, forming a barrier to the outside world, protecting them from prying eyes.

In another place, a different time, Harley would have marveled at the display of Dawn's wings unfurling. Right now, though, all Harley could think about was what waited for her at the edge of her grasp. With a little internal coaxing, she unsnapped Dawn's jeans. Hooking her thumbs in the waistband, she slowly, almost torturously, slid the pants to Dawn's hips, past her ass, and then hesitated. Harley was befuddled for a moment, losing her focus. Angels, or spiritual beings, wore underwear.

You're way overthinking this!

Sorry, I'm a little ADD right now.

Harley composed her thoughts, pushed away the intrusion, and let her body run on autopilot. Cupping Dawn's firm cheeks, she pulled Dawn against her. She squirmed as her own desire flooded her pants. She let her hands, one in the front and one behind, glide under Dawn's panties. She slipped her fingers between wet lace and hot body. Searching out the silky wetness of Dawn's lips, she gently touched Dawn's hard clit. Not moving fast enough, Dawn pressed Harley's hand against her and began rocking on it.

Stunned, Harley let Dawn slide a finger between the soft folds of her pussy and into her. Dawn arched away from Harley, pushing herself farther onto Harley's hand.

"More," Dawn whispered.

With practiced ease, Harley slipped another finger in and slowly and rhythmically worked them in and out of her lover.

Dawn covered Harley's mouth with her own, a moan slipping from Dawn's to Harley's. They fell into the tempo of practiced lovers. They were arching and bowing when suddenly Dawn's body rocked in orgasm over Harley, each tremor releasing another moan into Harley's mouth. Breathing in unison, they crashed together. Harley hugged Dawn as the weight of her body covered Harley's. Her huffs echoed in Harley's ear just as Dawn whispered, "I'm sorry."

"What?"

Harley wanted to push Dawn off, but her body reacted just the opposite and pulled her closer, tighter into her own space. Afraid, she couldn't look at Dawn. She worried that she'd see the same regret on her face that always accompanied a mistaken encounter. For some reason, she wouldn't be able to take that from Dawn, not tonight.

"I shouldn't have forced you." Dawn buried her head farther into the nook of Harley's shoulder. "I couldn't control how I feel about you, how I've always felt."

A moment of confusion flashed but then broke away from Harley's mind. "We've done this before, haven't we?" The answer to that question would answer so many suspicions Harley was feeling.

Harley pushed up and searched Dawn's face. It was true; they'd been lovers, but how?

Chapter Sixteen

Something warm brushed against Harley's nose. Dawn softly snored in her ear, the sweet breath a gentle reminder that they were locked in an embrace. It reminded her of a feather. Peering through a crack in her vision, Harley froze. A wing, at least that's what it looked like, was wrapped around her, like a blanket. With each breath Dawn took, the wing fluttered.

"Oh, Christ, what did I do?" Harley whispered.

"What? What's wrong?"

Harley couldn't face Dawn so she just lay on her side. How could she have made such a blunder? Sleeping with an angel. What was she thinking?

"I…I forgot you're…I'm sorry. I shouldn't have forced myself on you like this," Harley said, holding Dawn's arm tucked under her own.

Apparently stunned, Dawn flipped Harley and straddled her legs. In an instant, Dawn covered her breasts and pulled her wings in, hiding them from view. Then she quickly rolled off Harley and slipped her blouse on.

What was she doing? Dawn wasn't some chick she'd met in a bar. She was…different.

"What's wrong? Did I do something wrong?" Dawn eased away from Harley, resting against the haystack. Her aura eased from fuchsia to purple, and she covered her face, obviously embarrassed.

"No, no, not at all. It's me. I shouldn't have...I mean I, you're a...well, we're not from the same place. I'm just, well, I'm a human and you're...an angel, or something."

Harley reached out and drew Dawn tight against her chest. They had only hours, or maybe even just a few minutes, before all the madness started all over, and she wasn't any closer to understanding what she was mixed up in.

"Help me understand what's happening," Harley said. "I'm trying to grasp all of this, Dawn, but I'm struggling."

Dawn rolled back onto Harley's body. Resting her head on Harley's chest, she trailed a finger around a nipple and then plucked it playfully.

"I wish I could plug your brain into a computer and download everything, but it doesn't work that way, Harley." Dawn propped herself up on her elbows and pressed her finger to Harley's temple. "It comes in fits and starts. You'll remember this piece—like you did when you saw yourself with the sword."

"Can't we do some mind-meld kinda thing?"

Harley grabbed Dawn's finger and pressed it against her lips. Why couldn't it be easier? Did people who had past lives remember them? In some of those shows she'd seen on the Discovery channel, they were always interviewing some psychic who was telling people who they had been in a prior life. Why couldn't Dawn do that?

"Afraid not."

Harley brushed a strand of hair out of Dawn's eyes. She was beyond beautiful, but maybe the afterglow of sex was coloring her mind. Her classic Greek features pulled at Harley's heart.

"Then tell me who we're running from, because it feels like we're being chased."

Dawn evaded Harley's gaze and said, "We're trying to get Jack to his gate."

"Can I tell you something?" Harley asked. "Assuming you haven't already read my mind."

"Of course. You can tell me anything."

"I'm scared," she confessed.

"I wouldn't trust you if you weren't."

But there was something Dawn wasn't saying. Harley could feel it. "Dawn?"

Harley lifted Dawn's face and searched it for anything that looked remotely like agreement. She'd just spilled her guts to someone whom she'd only known for a few days, and

Dawn just sat there.

"Did you hear me?"

"Harley—"

Harley threw up one hand. "Wait. I know what's coming next. It isn't you. It's me. Blah, blah, blah."

Dawn grabbed Harley's hand and flattened it against her chest. "Can you feel that?"

Harley looked down at her hand on Dawn's chest and noticed a white tattoo similar to her own. It flashed of blue and then was gone. "Of course I can feel that. It's your heart beating." Harley blushed as she realized how fast Dawn's heart was pounding.

"I'm a guide, a guardian. I'm your guardian. My job is to help you get souls to the gate, to help you kill gatekeepers and keep some sort of balance on this side of the world. If I fall in love with you, what happens to my ability to do my job?"

"Let me guess. You're married to your work?"

Dawn ran a fingertip over Harley's fingers,

tracing an outline around Harley's hand. They looked at each other, and Harley's heart lurched. She wanted to kiss Dawn but hesitated. She could feel Dawn's energy flow into her, a sign she'd recognized lately. Dawn was heating up, her aura was vibrating again, and a light stream of blue enveloped them.

"That's funny, but I'm—" Dawn looked puzzled.

"I know, I know. You're an angel, and angels don't get involved with us mere mortals."

"Not exactly, but you're close."

Harley grabbed Dawn's hand and pressed it to her chest. "Do you feel that?"

Dawn arched an eyebrow and pursed her lips.

"Well, that's a beating heart. Someone who's alive and...well, let's just say I'm more than a little attracted to you." Harley held the hand tighter when Dawn tried to pull back from her. "Don't tell me you don't feel something too. Or am I being presumptuous?" Harley didn't think she was, but more than one woman had punted her because she assumed too much. Harley pulled Dawn's hand to her lips and gently placed a kiss on Dawn's palm. The spark nearly bowled Harley over.

"Sorry." Dawn's embarrassment colored her entire face as she spoke. "I can't seem to control these kinds of emotions. It's one of the reasons I don't get involved. Besides, female Protectors aren't that usual. Us being together would be a little clichéd, don't you think? The human-and-an-angel kinda thing"

"Not from where I'm sitting." Harley smiled. She had an arrogant streak that hadn't had a chance to show itself with all of the zigzagging they were doing between worlds, but in the quiet of this place, Harley felt protected. Dawn's guard was finally down, and she planned to take advantage of that simple fact.

"How many Paladins are there?" Were there many others like her? If so, how did they cope? How was their adjustment process? Would she be able to talk to them? Compare notes?

"Thousands."

"Can I see them?"

"Sometimes, but it's frowned upon for Paladins to gather in groups, except during the Gathering. If something were to happen to all of you, it would hurt the balance."

"Hmm." Harley was trying to digest the information Dawn was spoon-feeding her in small, digestible bites. "What's the Gathering?"

"It's a place where other Paladins meet, talk, share stories and experiences, and find some companionship for a brief moment."

Harley raised an eyebrow, encouraging Dawn to tell her more.

"It is an event where all the Paladins and their Protectors gather. Call it team-building older-world style."

"How old-world are we talking?"

"Guess it depends on whether you're a Protector or a Paladin. Most of us have been around from the beginning. Actually, all of us have been around from the beginning."

"When is this meeting?"

"When Mother calls it. If it was at a prescribed time the Dark Souls would know. There's always a Paladin who thinks about switching sides, who would tell the dark angels."

"Switching sides? You mean you can pick sides? Isn't your life preordained as a Paladin?"

"Once a Paladin recognizes their power, I

wish I could say it doesn't happen, but once they're empowered they can break with tradition and choose to work with the dark side."

Harley had never imagined there might be Paladins fighting with the Dark Souls. "But they're human and could see us. Isn't that dangerous?"

Dawn looked down at her hands, turning them over, and then returned her gaze to Harley.

"It is, and when we encounter such traitors, you must kill them. They tilt the scales in favor of the darkness, and they can't live."

Kill them?

Did she mean that Harley would have to kill another human being? How was that possible? She definitely wasn't signing up for murdering another living person. This was crazy shit. How would she know a Paladin was on the other side? She couldn't believe this job didn't come with some kind of training guide. Every damn job entailed some type of training. She tried to stop her runaway questions. There she went again, thinking in terms of the real world. Christ.

Impulsively, Harley blurted out, "What happens if I meet someone and want to have a family? Won't my being a Paladin put them at risk?"

The question appeared to startle Dawn. "Paladins can't have children. They can have a mom and dad— yes. Children—no. They would distract and cloud a Paladin's judgment and influence choices that they have to make."

"Lovely," she said, sarcasm lacing her retort. "What if something happens to you?"

"Nothing will happen to me."

"How can you be sure?"

"Harley, haven't you guessed by now...you and

I, we're connected. We've been together before." Dawn let her hand wander over Harley's chest. She playfully tweaked a nipple and then softly placed a kiss on Harley's neck. "I've waited for you for centuries."

Harley tried to wrap her mind around what Dawn was saying. Silence passed between them as Harley twirled a lock of Dawn's hair between her fingers. It was so soft. Her mind was shutting down. Harley couldn't remember the last time she'd slept. Oh, wait, back at the campground. How long had that been? Her eyelids drooped.

What had Dawn said? Centuries?

"I don't understand," Harley uttered as she drifted off to sleep.

⧉⧈⧉⧈

Shards of light sliced through the narrow slats of the barn wall. Dust particles floated in the air like spastic dancers. Harley tried to catch the dust fairies in her hand, but the impossible task reminded her of her childhood. She and her girlfriends would lie on the floor of her treehouse grasping at the minute particles, pretending that if they caught them a fairy would grant them a wish if they freed her.

Opening her own hand, Harley studied it, turning it over and tracing the veins with her finger. Realization hit her. These hands had saved lives. However, within a matter of hours, they'd taken five Dark Souls. She wrestled with a myriad of emotions: grief, hate, revenge, and the feelings of love she'd experienced last night. She still couldn't believe she and Dawn had spent a lifetime—no, lifetimes—together.

Closing her eyes, she let her soul slip into that

last thought.

Lifetimes.

Lovers.

How?

"Did you get your questions answered last night?" Jack asked.

A blush crept up her neck and heated her face. She couldn't look at him. He'd know something had happened. Guys always knew. Her whole crew had known when she crushed on the visiting deputy chief. Jack would realize she and Dawn had been intimate. Then she wondered how long Jack had been watching her marvel at the sight of her own fingers.

"No."

"If you ask me, I don't think they can be answered. You are what you are, Harley. You can go home and crawl back into your body and try to get on with life. But can you forget what you've seen here?" Jack sat up. "Honestly?"

Though Jack was a raving lunatic most of the time, this time he made a modicum of sense. "No, in your eyes, I don't suppose I can."

She thought about last night with Dawn. Could she give that up? Would she want to?

"You're a Paladin, a hero, Harley. Why can't you just accept that fact? I had to accept this." Jack pointed to his chest.

"I'm not some hero, so don't make me out to be one. If I'd had my way, you and I would have parted company a long time ago. Does that sound like a hero to you?" Her temper rose with each word.

"But you are, Harley. You didn't leave me behind. Oh, they won't write stories or sing songs about you, but you're a hero to those who need one. Just look at the profession you chose. You're a firefighter and a teacher. You save lives, mold young souls, and why?"

"Because I want to help people."

"Exactly. You want to help people who can't help themselves."

"This is different."

"Why?"

"It's life and death. If I screw up, someone might not make it to their gate and to their next life, their next choice." Harley hung her head.

Jack slapped Harley on the shoulder and rubbed her neck affectionately. "You're just not getting this, Harley."

"How's this for a news flash, Jack? I don't want to get this," she said, making air quotes around *get*. "This…" She threw her hands wide. "*This* isn't my idea of a life. Wandering around fighting off Dark Souls, killing gatekeepers, hoping we find your gate before some mythical creature catches us. *This* isn't my idea of fun."

"Are you done?" Dawn said, clearly not trying to hide the disappointment in her voice. "We're burning daylight, and the longer we take to get Jack to his gate the more likely it will be that Dark Souls will find us."

"That's just it, Dawn. As I was explaining to Jack, I'm not cut out for this type of work. I'm not some superhero. I'm just an average firefighter who likes to ride my motorcycle a little too fast. I also drink a little too much, and if I'm lucky with the ladies, I bag one." Harley picked herself and her pack up, slung it on her shoulders, and started walking toward the barn door.

She'd purposely flung that last line at Dawn. Now, glancing back and seeing the look on Dawn's face, she wanted to run to her, scoop her up, and leave in the opposite direction. Away from whatever evil what chasing them and hide from it.

"You can't hide, Harley. It's your destiny." Dawn's voice chilled the air.

"It's not my destiny if I don't choose it. Right? You can't make me be a Paladin. I have to decide if I'm going down that path. You," she pointed a finger at Dawn, "don't get to plan my life for me."

"You're right. We don't pick weak souls like you. A dog would be a better Protector than you, Harley. At least they know their place and who their master is, unlike horny losers like you." Dawn motioned for Jack, who stood with his mouth agape. "Paladins are proud, loyal, and fearless. You're more like a scared puppy that wets itself at a loud sound. Scurry home to your mommy so she can protect you. We have no room for pathetic whiners."

Dawn scoured Harley's body with hard eyes and sneered after her last comment. "To imagine I once loved you. Your fate is sealed. Keep a watch over your shoulder. The gatekeepers won't stop looking for you, Harley."

"Harley, please," Jack pleaded.

"It's done, Jack. We have to go." Dawn's anger flowed off her and slammed against Harley, pushing her out of the way. Not a lethal blow, but one that would leave a mark for a few days.

Calling Harley a coward was low, even for someone as pure as Dawn. If she'd meant for her words to sting, Dawn would never know how deep she'd penetrated Harley's armor. Her life around men at the station house had coarsened her. Their constant put-downs and jabs at being a woman had turned her insides into steel.

Dawn, though, knew just where to poke and what wound to stick it in. Like that wicked paper cut she'd gotten in the sixth grade. The damn thing had smarted even worse when she licked it. She'd learned a valuable lesson about how to handle paper out of the box. Don't slide your hand down it. Let it fall gently between your hands and then press it together. Handling women was pretty much the same way. Let them fall through your fingers, because the tighter you held on, the more pain they caused.

"This is your destiny. It's always been your destiny, Harley. It has been for centuries. Why can't you accept it?"

"I'm not some hero, so don't make me out to be one."

"But you are, Harley. You're one of those unsung heroes. Oh, they won't write stories or sing songs about you, but you'll be a hero to those who need one. Just look at the profession you chose. You're a firefighter. You save lives, and why?"

"Because I want to help people."

"Exactly. You want to help people who can't help themselves."

"This is different."

"Why?"

"It's life or death. If I screw up someone might not make it to their gate and to their next life, their choice." Harley hung her head.

"You're just not getting this, Harley."

Harley settled into the warmth soothing her soul.

"Harley, please."

"She's not coming, Jack. Stop wasting your time

on a mere mortal."

"Wait. You need to take me back to my car, or the hospital, somewhere. Don't you dare leave me out here." Her voice was colored with anger.

The hate from Dawn was palpable as she shook her head.

Harley grabbed Dawn's arm just as she and Jack were jumping.

Suddenly everything went black.

"Crap."

Chapter Seventeen

The crisp shades of oranges and reds streaked the dusk sky. Harley stood by herself, waist-deep in water. Turning in circles, she realized she wasn't where she started with Dawn and Jack. In fact, she couldn't see them anywhere. Somehow they'd become separated during the jump.

Turning, she surveyed her surroundings. Yep, she was stuck in God-only-knows-where-land.

"Christ, this sucks," she said, wading toward the bank. The last time she checked, things that could eat her swam in shit like this. She trailed her hand through the murky slush, worried she'd find a leech attached to it. The brown tinge gave her the willies. Pushing faster, she stumbled over a root, falling chest-deep into the muddy water.

"Fuck me."

Pushing her hand into the muck, she righted herself and sloshed to the bank again. This time she landed with a thud, knee-deep in mud and debris. Reaching for some grass, she slid back as the slimy lifeline slipped through her fingers.

"Can't I catch a break?"

Harley heard a splash behind her. The motivating sounds of something swimming toward her pushed her forward, crawling on her hands and knees over trash that littered the area. Slithering up the embankment, she slid to her back and pulled her gun from her waistband.

She pointed it forward. She could see a sheen of oil floating across the water, the waning sunlight revealing its toxic rainbow. Thankfully, she hadn't gotten any of the water in her mouth. Still watching, she didn't see anything breach the surface. Leeches were the least of her worries. Ripples from whatever had entered the water edged toward her, diminishing as they flowed closer to the shoreline. She wasn't taking any chances. Crab-walking backward, she hit a stump and stopped.

The heavy air around her buzzed with swamp life. Mosquitoes were trying to make a meal out of her neck. The familiar smell of smoke mixed with decay made her nose itch.

"Hello, Harley," a deep baritone voice oozed from behind her.

She froze. Her blood ran cold. This wasn't good. No one out here knew her. That only meant one thing, and it was all bad.

"I have a gun," she said, in hopes it would motivate the man behind her to change his mind, or whatever he had planned for her.

"I know," he said.

From the sound of it, or lack of it, he hadn't moved.

"I'd get out of the water if I were you."

Afraid to turn around, she froze. He knew who she was, and that meant danger.

"I would, but I'm not sure who's more dangerous—you or them."

She could pinch herself for being so sarcastic. Her mouth always engaged before her good sense did, and now she'd pay for it. Another splash and she was on her feet, her knife pulled from its resting place, blade out, her gun aimed behind her. She'd lucked out.

It was pointed right at the man. She could make out his form in the shadow of the overhanging tree. The red embers of a lit cigar cast a slight glow on his face. He puffed on the long stick, bringing it to life, then blew the smoke in her direction.

"How are you, Harley?"

"Do I know you?" She whipped around, sliding her knife hand under her gun hand, pointing the blade tip right at him.

He could see her, so obviously he wasn't a Dark Soul. That didn't mean he wasn't something worse.

"Ah, you do know me," he quipped. Another pull on the cigar and Harley could barely make out his features. The light of dusk turned to the beginning of darkness.

How poetic, Harley thought, watching him as she tried to remember if they'd met. His eyes were black—the kind of black that didn't reflect light but absorbed it.

"In this life, a time or two. I doubt you'd remember though." He blew on the tip of the cigar, creating a mini-blast furnace on the end of the stick. It lit him up enough that Harley could see a jagged scar across his face from the corner of his right eye, across his cheek, to the center of his chin. The raised skin was thick and smooth across the top.

Christ, that's vicious, she thought.

"Oh, this," he said, raking his nails across the taut skin. "A gift from a Paladin."

Her blood ran cold for a second time tonight.

He'd not only read her mind, but he'd also practically called her a Paladin. Only one person could read her mind, and she was probably halfway around the world with Jack.

"Where *is* Dawn?" he said around the stump of the cigar that kept her focused on his lit face. He half-smiled and pulled long and deep on the tobacco. Something told her she'd have to clear her mind of everything if she was going to survive this encounter.

"How is that sister of mine?" He smiled, white teeth, like clean snow, splitting his face in two, breaking the scar in half. Her look of confusion only added to his seeming delight in flustering her. "Oh, she didn't tell you? Well, you're just one of many of her playthings. I'm sure she just forgot to mention me. Ever since Mother tossed me out on my ass and back into Father's camp, Dawn's had a hard-on for me. You know, death and all." He exaggerated his movements and spread his hands wide. His fingers looked more like claws, with spikes at the end of each finger—deadly, she was certain.

"Aren't you curious about who I am?" he asked.

"Nope."

"You're afraid of me, aren't you?" He clapped his hands together in noticeable glee. "Oh, a Paladin who's afraid. That's rich."

The hair on her neck pricked as he continued his gloating. She wasn't afraid. She just needed to get her bearings and figure out what the hell was going on. He had surprise on his side, while she had a knife and a gun on hers. If she could kill a Dark Soul, she suspected she could kill this loud-mouth chatterbox of a demon. At least she suspected he was a demon. Nothing else fit.

"Oh, I'm sorry. I didn't tell you my name. How uncivilized of me," he said, extending his hand. White cuffs, complete with cufflinks, pushed out from a black sports coat. Completely out of place in the swamp, but at this point, nothing surprised Harley. "Alastor."

"Alastor," she repeated, but didn't shake his hand.

"I've gone by many names. In Slavic times, they called me, Rusalka. In Japanese folklore, they called me Oni. In Jewish myth, I'm known as Asmodeus. I actually just prefer to be called Al, but hey. I'll answer to almost anything."

"How about Gatekeeper? Do you answer to that?" It was a wild guess on Harley's part, but tonight she was into taking risky chances.

Harley took a sideways step as he spoke. Evil rolled from him in waves, almost sending Harley to her knees. Keeping her knife and gun in front of her, she followed him as he moved off the tree and into the moonlight.

"Well, I can see you aren't much for civility. Tsk, tsk, this younger generation. Always in a hurry. So uncultured."

With the full moon behind him, his large physique should have cast a huge shadow over her. Instead, he absorbed the light. Like a black hole, he just sucked it in, along with the energy around him. The spot he'd leaned against on the tree was dark and dead. The swamp grass around his feet died with each step. Harley continued to circle him, suspecting that if she touched him, her fate would be the same as the plants falling around him.

Looking for an escape route, she eyed the swamp to her right, then realized that the forest lay behind her. However, he was directly in front of her, trying to move closer with each tango step they did in unison. Lunge, volley, and next would be part. She didn't have a lot of options.

"So you never said how my sister was. Is she

well?" He tried once more. "Are you lovers again?"

Harley twisted her brow up and pinched her lips in a firm line. He, on the other hand, casually continued to walk in a circle. She didn't know who was stalking whom. Who was the prey and who was the attacker? His hands flailed around as he spoke, his lips never losing the cigar as he continued to talk around it. An occasional puff of smoke drifted upward, adding to the ring encircling his head.

"You know, my sister is quite charming. She gets it from me," he said, pretending to shine his nails on the velvet lapel of his smoking jacket. "I taught her everything she knows about women. She was a quick study. Really didn't need my help. The girl was a natural. Embarrassing, actually. Found ourselves going after the same women."

"Hmm," was all Harley offered. She wouldn't be distracted by his mindless banter. Even if he thought Harley would believe his bullshit, *he* didn't know Harley as well as he thought.

"You know coveting something is a sin, right?" Harley tossed out. Before she could say another word, a familiar voice spoke behind her, and someone touched her shoulder.

"Lucius, why am I not surprised?" Dawn stepped forward into Harley's view. If her look was any indication of the situation, Alastor, or Lucius, had something to fear.

"Sister, I wondered when you'd show up." He stepped forward, his arms open wide as if he might get a hug. Realizing there wasn't a chance in hell, he split his scar again and stopped, closer to Harley than she liked. "Your Paladin and I were just discussing you."

"Were you now?" Dawn stepped in front of

Harley, hands on her hips.

"You came back for me."

"Hardly."

"Did you two have a fight? Lovers' quarrel perhaps. She's always been hardheaded."

"Fuck you," Harley snarled.

"See. Nothing changes," Lucius said. A sneer etched its way across his face.

"I don't know who the fuck you are, so back off." Harley moved closer.

"Oh, but you do," Lucius said, running his finger down his scar. "We've met before, dear."

A vision of herself in some sort of leather armor, wielding a sword, flashed in Harley's mind. She watched as she plunged the sword through the heart of a Dark Soul. He vanished. She caught sight of a battle-ax swinging at her and dodged the swing that would surely have taken off her head. She felt the breeze it created as it passed. A scream behind Harley made her turn.

"Mother, run."

The woman stood in the doorway wearing a linen gown, her hand to her mouth, stifling another scream. Lucius stood behind her. He flashed an evil grin as their gazes locked. The glint of steel at her mother's neck had Harley running to save her.

She was too late as she caught her mother's body, falling to the ground.

"NO!"

"You should have joined me. I gave you fair warning." Lucius wiped his knife on her dress and then whispered in her ear. "You will come to me, girl."

Before Harley knew what she was doing, she lashed out at Lucius, her knife splitting his face from his cheek to his chin.

"You bitch." Lucius reached up and grasped his injury. Blood oozed between his fingers.

Harley looked down at her hand, the blade suddenly on fire. She dropped it. She didn't have time to wonder what had just happened. Her mother needed her. Scooping her up, she took her mother's body into the hut and gently laid her on the straw bed. Someone stood beside her.

Dawn.

"I'm so sorry, my child." Dawn's gentle voice wrapped her battle-wracked body.

"How could he do this? I thought Protectors weren't allowed to kill. Only protect."

"They're not allowed."

"Then how did this happen?" Harley held her hands wide over her mother's body.

"Your blade. You could have taken revenge on Lucius. Mother embedded it with enough power to kill him."

"That's how I was able to slice his face? I didn't know. If I had, he would have died tonight." Harley picked up her sword and sheathed her knife. One look back at her mother and she walked to the door.

"Where are you going?"

"To kill Lucius."

"Your mother needs a Paladin, child." Dawn closed her eyes and raised her hands to the skies. White light soaked the room, and her mother sat up.

Lucius would have to wait. Her mother needed a guide.

"I'll kill him. I swear on my mother's spirit he will die."

"Just not today." Dawn grabbed her mother's hand

and walked her toward Harley. "She needs you now."

Suddenly the vision was gone. She did indeed know this bastard. Stepping toward him, she pulled her knife but stopped as a voice boomed.

"Back off, Lucius."

Dawn pushed Harley behind her.

"I'm so glad you're here. I wanted to apologize about—" Harley said.

"Stop talking," Dawn said with a deliberateness Harley hadn't seen before.

"Wait. I'm trying to explain—"

"I'm not interested," Dawn whispered and then focused back on Lucius.

"Aw, you did have a lovers' spat. Not surprising, really. She can be a handful."

"Shut up, Lucius. Don't you have somewhere to be? Someone to terrorize?"

"Seriously, sister? I'm exactly where I'm supposed to be." Lucius spread his hands wide and smiled. "Besides, I have some unfinished business with our friend here."

Harley corrected him. "No, you don't. I don't even know who the hell you are." She *didn't* know him from a stranger walking down the street, but she sensed he was pure evil.

"Oh God, really?" He pushed forward and stood nose to nose with Dawn. "Her mind must be fried after all these centuries. Eventually, she'll be mine. You know that. I owe her."

"Is that why you've been sending so many of your minions after her? I mean, really, Lucius. You know the rules. You can't touch her. If you do, there will be hell to pay."

"Oh, you mean Mother. Well, she can't touch me and you know it. Besides, Father is pissed. You know he hates to lose the Dark Souls."

"Then you shouldn't be sending them after her. It's going to backfire on you, Lucius. Mark my words." Dawn kept pushing Harley behind her.

"Stop talking like I'm not here. I may not know what you're discussing, but I get the distinct idea that you and I are enemies, and we're going to settle whatever's between us over that little scar on your face."

Lucius snapped his pearly whites at her. Harley could see fangs. She pinched herself. She had to be dreaming. Wake the fuck up, she thought. Things had just gone sideways, and he wasn't just some pissed-off soul.

"Oh, it's no dream, sweetmeat." He leered at Harley, making her skin crawl.

Turning toward Dawn, Harley thought of something. "Where's Jack?" she whispered.

"He's safe, for now."

"Oh, my, an unprotected soul. My people must not be doing their job." Lucius laughed, his jaw bunched with tension. "It wouldn't be such a problem if your Paladin here wasn't so proficient at killing my darling minions."

"I've only killed those that needed killing. Maybe you need to rein those bastards in, or they—"

"Don't." Dawn held her hand up and stopped Harley.

A water drop hit Harley and then another, and suddenly she was drenched. Lightning streaked across the sky, just as a clap of thunder rattled her bones.

"Great. Can't I just catch a break here?"

Without thinking, Harley pulled the collar of her jacket up and yanked her hat from her backpack. She pushed it on and held her backpack over her head.

"So what happens now?" Harley asked. However, no one was around to answer her. Dawn and Lucius were gone.

"Dawn, wait. We need to talk." Harley reached for where Dawn had been standing only seconds before. Her heart sank. She'd opened her mouth without thinking, and now she wondered if she'd made the right decision.

She was standing alone with no idea exactly where. Remembering what Dawn had said, she realized that Protectors and Paladins had regions. At least that meant Harley was in *her* region. Turning in a circle, Harley spotted a small trail. Probably an animal trail, but it was something. Each step would take her back to her body, and right now, that was all she wanted—

to get back to normal. Whatever that was.

Chapter Eighteen

Harley didn't know where she was, and she didn't care. Bum-fuck nowhere was fine. Dawn and Jack had bolted on her, or was she the one who'd told them to kick off? No matter. She wasn't who they thought she was, and that was fine with her.

Harley shoved the door, almost knocking it off its hinges.

"Whoa there, Hulk. It's just a door." A woman standing there holding a coffeepot and wearing a waitress's uniform looked like she was right out of the fifties.

"Sorry." That was all Harley could offer as she realized everyone was staring at her.

After last night, with Dawn throwing her to the darkness, Harley had to be honest—she was shocked. Hadn't Dawn told her they were soul mates? Clearly another overused descriptor in any century.

"Piss off," Harley whispered.

"Excuse me?"

"Nothing." Harley knew she was coming off as a lunatic, so she'd better get herself together. She didn't need any more trouble than she already had. Looking around the diner, she found it weird that they could see her. The door had girth, and she was actually starving, tired, and angry. She'd spent her time lately chasing shadows and walking *around* the living. Now she was back in their world, as if she'd never left.

Sliding onto a chair at the counter, she shifted her hips, pulled her wallet out of her front pocket, and thumbed through the bills. She had enough for something to eat and maybe a roach motel later.

"What can I get ya, hon?"

"The biggest cup of coffee in the place."

"Only comes in one size, but refills are on the house."

She smiled down at Harley. The name tag said Gert. Funny, she didn't look like a Gert.

"Menu?"

"Only got a few things, and they're right there on that chalkboard over there." Gert pointed to the daily listings that didn't seem to have changed for a while. The only evidence of change was the ghosted-out prices replaced with newer ones.

"Okay." Harley checked out the limited items. "Burger, fries, and pancakes." She hadn't smoked in years, but she suddenly had the urge for a cigarette. "You sell cigarettes?"

Gert nodded. "Vending machine outside, around the corner. Pick up your butts, and I'll call ya when your order's up."

"Thanks."

The waitress tossed Harley a book of matches. Catching them, Harley noticed the diner's tagline, THE HOTTEST SPOT NEXT TO HELL!

Harley spotted a TV hanging in the corner of the diner. News crackled through the poor reception, touting the latest doom and gloom. Ignoring it, she asked the waitress, "Can I leave my backpack here?" She pointed to it on the floor.

"Sure, hon. No one here'll bother it. Take your coffee and relax. I'll call ya when supper's ready."

Gert sounded more like her mom than a waitress. Harley wondered what her mom was doing at that very moment. *Probably sitting by my bedside in the hospital.*

"Thanks."

The bell rang when she pulled the door. Funny she didn't remember hearing it when she'd shoved through earlier.

Harley reached into her pocket and pulled out a wad of bills and some change.

Fuck me, she thought. Counting out four quarters, she pulled the lever for the Reds and watched a five-pack of cigarettes drop to the bottom.

Of course, a baby pack of smokes. She'd seen these before at the bowling alley, when her folks took her with them on bowling night. She pulled the minipack and twisted the cellophane pull from the top. As she jerked one out of the wrapper, it disintegrated before she got it out all the way.

"Shit."

She pulled another, and then finally a third came out intact but bent. "If I didn't know better, I'd say the world is sending me a message."

"Why is that?" the waitress said behind her.

Startled, Harley grumbled to herself, "No reason. Just been my luck lately."

She put the filter to her lips, cradled the match, and pulled on the cigarette as she lit it.

"You know those things will kill you, right?"

"Somehow I think this"—she held up the cigarettes and blew smoke away from the waitress—"is the least of my worries. Trust me."

Topping off Harley's cup, the waitress nodded. "Your order's up. When you're ready."

"Thanks."

Harley sat at the outdoor table, tucked her legs under her, and leaned on her thighs. Looking around, she decided she could have been anywhere in Middle America, USA. A ding at the gas station across the street brought a man running to a station wagon at the pumps. Polite chatter between the two meant they knew each other. She watched as he cleaned the windshield, holstered the pump, and took cash from the man behind the wheel.

The driver looked over Harley and waved. Something about him shocked her. Before she could look again, he was gone. He cruised through the only blinking stoplight in town. The light was strung across the intersection, and it bounced like a stiff breeze caught it as the man passed under it. Funny that there wasn't even so much as a leaf moving in the heavily tree-lined street.

"Hey, food's getting cold," the waitress said, poking her head through the door.

"Thanks."

Harley watched the fading taillights until she couldn't see them anymore. She puffed a few more times before she stubbed the cigarette on the ground. Picking up the butt, she considered dumping the pack. Instead, she pushed it down in her back pocket and palmed the matches.

Taking her seat at the bar, Harley noticed that the TV crackled louder in the corner as a stocky man, in a stained apron, adjusted the makeshift tinfoil rabbit ears.

"That better?"

"It don't matter. Hell, only thing on, and it's that shit in San Francisco. Damn hippie commies," an old guy said, poking at his plate.

"What happened?"

"Where you been? Under a rock?"

"Off the grid" was all Harley offered.

"Got one of those eco-disasters over there in San Francisco."

"Eco-disasters?"

"Birds everywhere. Dead ones floatin' in the bay. Launching themselves into buildings."

"No. Not all buildings, Hank. Just the hospital," Gert corrected the man still trying unsuccessfully to avoid looking at the squawk box.

"Hospital?" Harley stared down at her plate.

"Crazy bastards. Probably all that pesticide. Nuttier than a PayDay."

"PayDay?" Harley said.

"You know the candy bar. Geez, girl, where'd you grow up?"

"Leave her alone, Hank. We aren't all news junkies like you." The waitress poured more coffee into Harley's cup. "Don't pay any attention to him."

"I wasn't. How long has that been going on?" Harley blew into a cup, took a sip, and then watched the news report out of the corner of her eye.

"Just after that freak storm blew through. They think the birds' radar got all discombobulated or something." Gert looked at the TV and crossed her arms, the nearly empty coffeepot hanging by two fingers. "Might be something to what Hank said. All those pesticides in the ground. The drought. Now all this rain." Putting the pot in the maker, she said, "But who knows? Things just get weirder and weirder, if you ask me."

With that, she pushed through the kitchen door, leaving Harley to her food. After smothering her pancakes with syrup, she cut them up and pushed them to the side. Picking up a few fries, she dragged them through the pool of syrup, popped them into her mouth, and then sighed. *Fuck the world.* She was going back to her old life and forgetting the last few days like a bad hangover.

Popping a few more greasy fries, she realized that junk had never tasted so good.

She studied the small screen and watched a reporter duck as a Raven flew right at her. Harley knew what the birds meant. They weren't playing kamikaze at just any hospital. Suddenly, she wasn't in such a hurry to get back to her body. A night in a hotel, another meal, and she'd have enough energy to figure out how she was going to make her miraculous entrance. Right now, though, she wanted to tune out the world at large. Forget about the guy in the station wagon and eat what was probably the best greasy burger of her life.

"Is there a motel in this town?" Harley said around her burger.

"Yep, only one. It's not the greatest, but it's clean, most of the time."

"Thanks."

"Better get there before Billy pulls the shade down. Once that's down, he's off, and ain't nothin' bringing him to the door."

"Hmm."

Harley leaned back and looked in the direction Gert has just pointed. A busted motel sign with a neon OPEN hung in the window. It was better than nothing at this point. All Harley wanted was a shower and a bed. Everything else was moot at this point.

"Tell 'em I sent ya and he'll give you the deluxe room." Gert refilled Harley's coffee. "It's a deal we have. I send 'em and he rents 'em." Gert's laugh echoed in the back as she hipped her way through the kitchen door.

Something was just creepy about this town. Just creepy.

Chapter Nineteen

Harley slogged across the dirt parking to the motel. More like the Bates motel, if you asked her. A beat-up Rambler had a layer of dust on it so thick, the WASH ME carved onto the windshield had a layer of dust covering the writing. A Grand Torino that had seen better days sat at the opposite end of the rutted dirt parking lot, and a brand-new, sparkling white Escalade sat right next to the front doors.

Harley had seen the man starting to pull the shade as she entered the shabby lobby, so she ran to the door and frantically pounded on the door, rattling the OPEN sign on a chain.

"You made it just in time," he yelled across the lobby, leaving the shade up.

"Gert sent me. Said when the shade was down you don't rent rooms. Said to tell you to give me the deluxe room."

"Did she?"

"Yep."

She pushed through the door and right into a scene from a B movie. The lobby reeked of body odor, stale coffee, and…Harley sniffed the room…piss. The sleazy motel with a broken sign. A motel manager in his two-sizes-too-small wife beater that was stained from his last week of meals. A sign-in book that he twisted toward her, his stubby finger pointing to an open slot.

"Got ID?"

Harley fished her wallet from her back pocket and tossed her driver's license at him.

"Got a credit card?"

"I'll pay cash."

"Need it for long-distance phone calls."

"I ain't making any. Turn the phone off if you want."

From what she gathered through the rest of his guttural groans, checkout was at ten a.m. instead of noon. Hot water for the shower was hit or miss, depending on who got it first, which made Harley look down the row of rooms. No cars were parked in front of them, so she wondered about the early checkout time and the hot water and didn't worry too much about either rule.

"Key?"

He tossed a giant plastic fob with a number on it. Number 10. All the way at the end of the line of rooms. Well, at least it wasn't upstairs.

"The fridge in the room doesn't work so—"

"Already ate."

"Good. We don't allow food in the rooms. Brings in mice and roaches."

The man tried to pull the fraying shirt down over his rotund stomach, as if he was suddenly embarrassed when she looked at his gut.

"You mean you don't already have 'em?" Harley muttered.

"Huh?"

"Nothing."

"Coffee and Danish in the morning here in the lobby."

A ceramic percolator stood sentry on a long table in the corner. She hadn't seen one of those since her last visit to her grandmother's house. In fact, the décor reminded her of that 70s'-something show. The only thing missing was a shag rug, a cluster of plastic grapes, and a hanging chandelier in the corner. *Then*, it would be her grandmother's house.

"Honey bear, make us some microwave popcorn," a gravelly voice yelled from behind the curtain.

Harley could only imagine the kind of woman on the other side of that fragile barrier.

"Honey bear?"

"In a minute," he yelled back.

Sliding the plastic fob closer to Harley, he grunted, "All the way down at the end. Don't forget checkout is ten."

"I won't forget." Harley palmed the fob, shouldered her backpack, and stepped into the pouring rain. She'd be shocked if she lasted—she peered at her watch—the ten hours till eight a.m.

Keying the lock, she had to shoulder the door open. Then she had to turn her head from the obnoxious heat and smell that poured out of the room.

"If this is deluxe, I'd hate to see what the standard room is."

Flipping the light on, she wished she hadn't. She should have known that if the lobby was a seventies' reject, her room wasn't going to be much better. The floral-print duvet, if that's what you could call the frail covering, had burn stains all over it. Tossing it off the bed only made matters worse. The sheets looked like they'd been slept in and the duvet just thrown over the bed to cover them.

"Christ."

Afraid to go into the bathroom, she picked up the phone and rang the front desk.

Ring.

Ring.

Ring.

Ring.

"Oh, this is bullshit," she said, almost ready to hang up just as someone came on the phone.

"Yeah?"

"Yeah, this is room ten. I need another room. Someone's already slept in this one."

It was quiet on the other end as she heard someone cover the mouthpiece.

"Are you sure?" the female voice asked.

"I know when a bed has been slept in, lady. Besides, this one smells like shit."

Again the woman covered the mouthpiece and said something to the manager.

"He'll meet you at room five. Just leave the key in the room, and Maria will get it day after tomorrow when she cleans."

"Whatever."

Gingerly, she picked up her backpack, then inspected it to make sure there weren't any hitchhikers on her stuff. Swatting the base, she slung it over her shoulder and beat feet to get out of the biohazard and slammed the door behind her. The rain was coming down harder now, so she hugged the wall as she walked down to room five. The wind started to pick up and push the rain directly at her against the wall. Pulling her hood on, she looked down at the office. No manager, yet.

"This is some bullshit."

She'd started walking toward the office when he

popped out of the door. A garbage bag with arms and a hat was walking toward her. She felt a laugh start but bit her lip. The manager grumbled all the way down to her door, jangling keys. Slipping one in, he twisted it, but no luck. Trying another, he tossed a curse word or two in her general direction and turned the key. Again, no luck. The rain was pelting them both as she stood watching him go through the complete ring of keys. She counted twenty-five, with only four more to go. Her luck it would be the last key…

"There you go." He pushed the door in and waved her through it.

"Hold on. You aren't going anywhere. If this room sucks, you're gonna find me one that's decent, and I use that term liberally, considering the last room."

"Yeah, sorry about that. I guess I forgot someone had used it for a couple of hours earlier." A blush crawled up his neck and colored his cheeks.

Gross. She didn't even want to imagine him with another woman, doin' the nasty.

She stepped inside and twirled around the room. She pulled the duvet back. Clean sheets. At least the bed was made. Walking into the bathroom, she saw that it had your standard miniature bottles of soap, shampoo, and conditioner. She bent down and sniffed the towels.

Bleach.

Flipping the TV on, she grabbed a washrag and pushed the buttons on the remote. Static.

"The storm, it takes the satellite out all the time. Should be on in a few minutes," he promised.

"It'll do."

"Checkout's still ten a.m."

"Right."

She slammed the door behind him and tossed her bag on the bed. God, what she wouldn't do for a drink.

Chapter Twenty

Harley clutched her chest. Her birthmark was on fire. Running her fingertips over her skin, she pulled back at the heat coming off her body. She twisted herself in the sheets, trying to get out of the balled-up linens. Extracting herself, she kicked the mess to the floor. Was she having a heart attack?

Impossible.

She stared up at the ceiling, trying to clear her mind.

Slow in.

Slow out.

In.

Out.

Harley.

She didn't move.

Harley.

Closing her eyes, she pulled the pillow over her head. Visions of Dawn danced behind her eyelids. Her mind was running in one loop. Dawn, hovering over her pressing her lips to her birthmark. Amazingly, her lips were almost the exact shape of the wine stain. Dawn, her wings flourishing into a full spread. Dawn, her face as she climaxed.

She could feel Dawn pressing herself against her. Passion flared as Harley reacted instantly. Heat pulsed through her veins. She reached up to cup Dawn's breasts as they bobbed before her.

Harley.

There it was again. The vision faded and she froze. The voice's pitch had changed to a baritone, and this time it was more taunting.

Harley.

Opening her eyes, she tossed the pillow off and searched the shadows of her room. God, why couldn't the voices in her head leave her alone just for a moment so she could sleep?

Harley.

Christ.

She shifted at whatever moved to her side.

Harley.

"God, I'm never going to sleep again, am I?"

Harley.

"What? Get the fuck out of my head and give me some peace," she said as she swung her legs off the bed. Resting her elbows on her knees, she cupped her hands over her ears, rocked back and forth, and started humming. She wanted to drown out the noise blaring in her head.

Harley.

Anxiety lanced through her. The thought of never sleeping again freaked her out. Sleep had been the one thing that helped her cope with her job. A great day was staying at home in her pajamas watching movies and fading in and out of consciousness as she binged on junk food.

Standing, Harley paced the room. Suddenly the walls were closing in on her. Maybe a walk around the parking lot would help ease her nerves. After searching for her jeans, she slipped them on and pushed her feet into her shoes, not bothering to lace them. She wasn't going to be out long. Hopefully.

The crinkle of cellophane caught her attention. Reaching down, she picked up the two cigarettes.

A smoke. Maybe that would help. Didn't it always work that way in the movies? The hero takes a walk, smokes a cigarette, and comes back with all the answers. Right?

Patting her pockets, she pulled the matches and read the flap again.

THE HOTTEST PLACE NEXT TO HELL!

"Hotter than hell. Yeah, I'm in hell all right."

Popping one in her mouth she almost lit up until she saw the plastic no-smoking sign on the table.

"Great. It's not like they'd notice."

Pulling the door open, she lit the tip and took a long, deep drag.

"Well, about time. I was starting to think I'd lost my touch." The baritone voice from her dreams rocked her to attention.

"Shit, not you again?"

Lucius leaned against the station wagon she'd seen earlier. Tapping the fender, he smiled. "Like it? I bet it brings back memories, doesn't it?"

Now that she looked at it, she had to admit it looked just like the one her dad had when she was a kid. Down to the painted hubcaps.

"Isn't it a little late for a social call, Allistor, Lucius, or whatever they call you?"

"Let's just say I knew you wouldn't be able to sleep tonight."

He was creepy in his metrosexual, perfect hair, over-tan looks, with his well-manicured but too-long-nails-for-a man kind of way. He reminded her more of a strutting peacock than the evil deity he tried to present. He rolled his cigar between his thumb and two fingers before he looked up at her.

"What do you want, Lucius?"

Harley pulled a long drag from her cigarette, acting like she couldn't care less that he'd been standing outside her room calling her. She stared at him and slowly let the smoke ease out of her nostrils. If he was trying to scare her, it wasn't working. Aggravate her, yes. For some reason she wasn't afraid. After everything she'd been through in the last twenty-four hours, the element of surprise wasn't on his side.

"What do you want from me, Lucius?"

"You," he said, blowing a cloud of smoke into the air that looked like a nuclear mushroom cloud compared to her little puff.

"Me."

"I want you to join my team, Harley."

Harley raised the cigarette to her lips and sucked in a short puff, then blew it in a thin stream in his direction. So he was going with that line instead of killing her. Oh, wait, he couldn't touch her. Maybe that was why she wasn't afraid of him. There was a hands-off policy on Paladins. Well, she wasn't a Paladin, but he didn't know that, yet.

"I'm not a team player, Lucius. Besides, I'm not your type." Harley flicked her cigarette off into a puddle and turned to leave.

"You don't get it, do you?"

"What am I not getting, Lucius?" She said his name in every sentence just to piss him off.

"Once you're out of the closet, so to speak, you can't go back in, Harley. You can try to go back to your old life, but…"

"But what?"

"Well, you'll always see Dark Souls. Do you

remember that movie where that kid saw dead people? It's kinda like that. You'll always see Dark Souls, and me, of course." He smiled, his tongue flicking off his fang.

Harley stood frozen. Was this her new normal?

"What's wrong? Dawn didn't tell you?" He slid off the fender and walked toward her.

"Stay away from me." She put up her hands and took a step back.

"Surely this can't come as a shock. I mean…what did you think would happen after you killed my people and screwed my sister?"

"For some reason, I just want to kill you, Lucius."

"I know. Isn't it great? Can't you just feel the evil building inside of you?" He smiled around his cigar and pumped his elbow back like he'd just dropped a hole in one on the eighteenth tee. As he blew another cloud into the darkness, she suddenly wanted to shove his cigar down his throat. "I can give you things, Harley."

Looking at the wreck of a ride he was leaning on, she chuckled. So, he thought she could be bought. Better people than he had tried and come up empty. Surely he knew that, assuming, as he said, he could see her past.

"Oh, like a station wagon?" She enjoyed mocking him.

He snapped his fingers, and the car changed to a sleek red Ferrari. "Maybe this is more to your liking."

She crossed her arms and shook her head. "Not interested."

He snapped his fingers again and a blonde appeared, wrapping herself around the deity.

"Hello, lover," she said, slipping her hand inside his shirt and hiking her leg up against his thigh seductively.

"Isn't this a little juvenile even for you, Lucius?"

He snapped his fingers again and another woman appeared. She lay prone on the hood of the Ferrari and arched herself as she growled and batted her eyes at Harley.

"Hello," she purred as she spread her arms across the hood, pushed her chest out, and then motioned to Harley to come closer.

"Maybe if I were a sixteen-year-old male, this would get my vote. Still not interested."

"Perhaps I can help you relax."

Sliding off the car and sauntering over to Harley, the blonde slipped her hands under Harley's shirt. Then she grabbed Harley's waist and yanked her hips against Harley's.

"Meet Ms. November. Sexy, aye?"

"Still not interested," Harley said, pushing Ms. November back. "It's not you, sweetheart. It's me."

"Oh, come on, Harley. It's bad taste to refuse a gift."

Lucius bent down and kissed the blonde, his mouth practically devouring her. "Well, you can't get any hotter that this smoky number. She makes Dawn look like a schoolgirl. And she's well equipped to handle all your desires. Aren't you, honey?"

"Any desire," Ms. November said, wrapping herself around Harley.

"Stop," Harley yelled. "You just don't take no for an answer, do you?"

A crack of thunder, and the women and the Ferrari were gone.

"Maybe you need a reminder of who I am and how powerful I am," Lucius growled. His mood had flipped. He waved his hand, and suddenly Harley was standing in a battle scene of sorts.

"Daughter, where have you been? I've been worried sick."

Harley looked down at her clothing from a different time. A basic linen gown, sandals, and hair ornaments adorned the other woman. Harley wore a leather pleated skirt and a breastplate, a sword hung at her waist. She didn't recognize the woman, but she didn't have time to find out who she was before a scream ripped through the area.

"Daughter, what's wrong? Where are your brothers?"

"Brothers?"

"Have you an injury, daughter?" A panicked look swept across the woman's face.

"Oh, come on, woman. Don't tell me you don't recognize your own mother?" Lucius's voice rang in her ears.

Spinning, she searched for the asshole. He stood in the doorway of a shack, arms crossed, with that smug look on his beautiful face. Only now, he didn't have a scar. His hair was longer, small ringlets around his forehead framing his face. He truly didn't change, did he?

"Mother?"

"Yes, dear. Are you all right?"

Her mother rushed toward her, grabbed her hands, and turned the empty one over. "Are you hurt? You have blood on them."

"I don't know."

Panic pulsed through Harley; she needed to get her mother inside, fast.

"Where are we and who's attacking us?"

Harley pushed her mother forward toward the door. "Mother, please," she said as the woman resisted.

"Your brothers, what news do you have of them?"

Thinking quickly, Harley answered, "We were split up. They went to the west, and I came back here to make sure you were okay."

"It's the king's men, daughter. They are looking for..."

"For?"

The woman's eyes widened, her mouth agape. Slowly, her finger rose to point at someone behind her.

Without thinking, Harley pulled her sword and made a turning, sweeping motion at the person, or persons, behind her. The tip of her blade was a shade of blue she'd never seen as it bisected the face of the man behind her. His eyes darkened, but he didn't move. Blood seeped down his face. His stare never leaving Harley's, he raised his hand, but not in Harley's direction.

Her mother's.

A shrill cry pierced the smoky air that was creeping over the ground. For a split second, Harley could only wonder if it would engulf her. Rushing to her mother, she caught the woman before she hit the ground. Falling to her knees, she cradled her mother's head in her lap.

"*Poneron.*" Her mother pointed to Lucius standing in the doorway. It was the Greek word for evil. How did she know that?

"Mother, stay with me, please."

"Find your brothers and kill Poneron. Promise me, daughter."

Harley doubled over and hugged her mother's body. A giant void filled her as her mother took a deep breath. Harley's breath escaped her. Her heart was squeezed in grief as she rocked her mother, the daughter taking the place of the mother at that moment. Harley let out a wail as her body vibrated quickly with hate.

"I will. I promise to avenge you…" Harley raised her head, arched her neck, and screamed, "Mooootttthhhhheeeeerrrrr."

"Well done," Lucius said, clapping. "A performance equal to any found at the theatron. Well done, girl." He leaned down and put his hand on the dying woman, her spirit rising above her. She looked at Harley, despair evident in her eyes. Without thinking, Harley picked up her sword and pierced Lucius through the hand.

"You will not take her soul, Poneron." Harley stood. Lucius's hand still impaled, she moved him against the wall, her strength beyond human as she pinned him. "I will kill you for this. I won't let you take my mother's soul."

"Daughter?" her mother's soft voice whispered behind her.

Pushing her sword farther, Harley put the tip under his chin. Blood from the wound she had served earlier was still seeping down his face. She didn't see fear, only death.

"You think you have me? I assure you that it is only a façade."

"Lucius, what have you done?" A woman's voice behind Harley blended with her mother's weeping.

"Goddess, my daughter. Please save her from Poneron. Please, Goddess."

"Ah, if it isn't Aphrodite's handmaiden. Sister. You really need to find another soul to save. This one is mine." Poneron sneered.

"I don't think you've looked at the situation realistically, Devil."

Poneron pushed his hand farther down the blade and away from his face, toward Harley.

"I think—"

Harley grabbed the blade with her other hand and pushed it back into his neck, nicking the skin.

"*Alala*. Please take your mother's soul to her gate." The goddess behind her spread her hands, wings spreading out behind her, and the most beautiful white and blue aura vibrated through the room. A sense of protection coursed around them, bouncing off the walls of the small hut.

Who are you? Harley let the question flow without conscious thought.

Your Protector. Now run.

Energy surged through the room, and all Harley could do was stand her ground as Poneron let a laugh and gave her a wicked smile, but with only part of his mouth. The other half couldn't comply since it was on the other side of the blade slice.

"You should listen to my sister. If not, it could be the last thing you do in this lifetime."

"I'm not done with you yet."

"It will take more than a new Paladin like you to take down a god like me, Alala. Besides, your mother's soul is in desperate need of protection. Look." He nodded behind her.

A man dressed as a centurion, who was also transparent, had pulled his sword and was bearing down on her mother. Things were jumbled in her mind. *Kill the god and no one else dies.* At least she hoped that was the way it worked. Or kill the centurion and take her mother to her gate. What was a *gate*? Now that her mother was dead, she didn't how it was possible to see her spirit. Things didn't make sense. Perhaps battle fatigue was setting in?

"Alala, hurry. You must protect your mother's spirit, or she won't be able to return in a later life and finish her work," the goddess said.

"You kill the centurion. You're standing right there," Harley yelled.

"I can't."

"What?"

"She can only protect you. That's why you're not dead by my hand." Lucius spit blood all over Harley as he laughed. "You Paladins are really—"

"Shut up, you devil. Clearly, I can kill you though." She pushed the blade farther into him.

"Your mother won't get a chance to come back, woman. The thread she started here will unravel, and your line of Paladins will be lost forever. So, what do the fates have in store for you?"

"He's right, Alala. You must protect your mother. Hurry." The goddess stood beside Harley. "Your bloodline must go on."

It was Dawn.

Chapter Twenty-one

Harley fell to her knees, sobbing. Scattered around her were memories, like pictures tossed randomly at her feet. As she reached for one, it disappeared the moment she touched it. Reaching for another, her fingers scratched the dirt.

"The pit in your stomach, that hole in your heart, is death," Lucius said, kneeling beside her. "Reach for another, Harley. Go ahead."

Harley curled into herself, feeling the visceral pain. The ache was so deep, she thought she might throw up.

"Get the fuck away from me, you bastard," Harley said, pushing him away.

"It hurts, doesn't it? Being a Paladin is hard, especially when you lose your mother. By the way, how *is* your mother?"

Harley sprang up, grabbing Lucius by the neck and squeezing. "You touch her and I'll kill you. Seems I have that power." Before she could stop herself, she ran her tongue up the scar on his face. "Or have you forgotten about this little gift?"

Lucius put his hands on her wrists and tried to dislodge her from his neck, merely making Harley squeeze harder.

"No one is coming to save you this time, asshole. Dawn is beyond pissed with me, and the last I heard, you had no one to protect you from me."

She wanted to laugh in his face, but her pain etched its way through her soul. The memories had taken their toll, and now she knew why she was reclusive and untrusting.

More memories tried to push themselves to the front, but she had to shove them back. If they were anything like the last bout, she'd be catatonic in a matter of minutes. She was on a mission, and that was to get home and protect her own family.

Her mission had become clear. It wasn't to stop the Dark Souls. It was to kill their gods. He was first on her list.

"Brother, I see you've gotten yourself into another mess." A tall woman draped in leather stood at the head of Harley and Lucius, who were now wrestling for dominance on the ground.

Harley planted her knee firmly on Lucius's chest and looked at the woman, who was oozing sex. Her attraction was instant. The woman had dark, short, spiked hair; flawless olive skin; and the most striking whiskey-brown eyes. God, she was gorgeous. Harley was sure she had left a trail of broken hearts behind her, not to mention souls that might mistakenly take a chance on all that seething sexuality. Not sure what side she played for, Harley cautiously kept her distance.

"Hello?" the woman said.

"Sister, be a sweetheart and get this Paladin off me."

"What've you done now, Brother dear?"

"Just a stroll down memory lane. Seems she didn't like the trip."

"Made another enemy, have you, dear?"

Lucius looked at Harley and offered an explanation for his sister. "She swings both ways, metaphorically and justice-wise too. Seems she can't pick a side when it comes to light and dark. Hence her fantastic personality." He looked back up at his gorgeous sister. "Now if you don't mind." His hand struggled against Harley's tightening grip.

The woman snapped her fingers, and he morphed out of her grasp and stood by the Ferrari.

"It's great to have a goal, Harley, but you can't kill me."

"Watch me."

She stood, her feet planted, her fists ready for battle. She stared at him and then at his sister. She'd have to be smarter, more cunning and deadly if she was going to kill them both.

"Alleo, meet Harley. Harley, meet my sister Alleo. Goddess of the Storm." Lucius scrubbed his neck.

"Hello, Harley. Nice to make your acquaintance." Alleo stuck her hand out. "Friends call me Allie. I hope we can be friends," Allie said, studying Harley's body before looking at her.

"Not likely."

"She's Dawn's sister."

"Ah, how is my sister?"

"I wouldn't know."

"Had a lovers' spat," Lucius said.

"Oh, my, that is tragic. Perhaps I can help." She stepped closer and offered her hand again.

"Sister, please. I call dibs." Lucius pulled Allie back.

"I think she may be…" Allie turned toward her brother and clasped her hands together, realization clearly dawning on her. "Oh. She's the one who gave you this, isn't she?" Allie ran her finger down Lucius's scar. "Brilliant." Allie turned about to Harley and said,

"I love her already. Grrr!"

"Excuse me." Harley stepped back and reminded them she was standing right here.

The rain started to fall again, light at first and then gradually growing heavier. Drops created bigger puddles of mud. Without saying anything, Harley turned and walked to her room.

She was done with this nonsense. She'd have her day with Lucius, but Allie… She had her firing on all cylinders, and that wasn't good.

Sexy evil meets slayer.

Not a good mix.

Her hand on the doorknob, Harley yelled over her shoulder at the gossiping pair. "How many of there are you?"

Silence.

Suddenly, Harley felt Allie press her body against her. "Why?" One hand slipped below the waistband of her jeans while the other traveled up Harley's shirt. The onslaught made Harley struggle to keep herself on her feet. "Show me your birthmark? I heard a super Paladin was released recently on Earth. I guess you're the one everyone is talking about." Her hand traveled to the birthmark, which flashed instantly, giving Harley away.

"Hmm, now aren't you the yummy one."

"How many are there of you?"

"Again, why the curiosity?"

Grabbing the hand in her jeans, she stopped its further travels. "Because I want to know how many of you I'm going to have to kill to right the balance in this world."

Allie slipped her tongue along the rim of Harley's ear, shooting a zing of passion straight to her center.

God, this was going to be hard.

Think of Dawn.

Think of Dawn.

"Are you stuck on my little sister? I can give you so much more than my lily-white sibling can. Trust me. I can fill your nights with passion and your days with slaying. You did just call yourself a slayer, didn't you?"

Harley would have to remember to keep her mind clear when the gods were around. What was that thing they'd tried to teach her in counseling? Meditation. Something like that.

"So, are you going to tell me how many there are of you, or should I just be surprised when I reach the end of the line?"

"You're cute, you know that?" Allie turned Harley around and pinned her to her door. "There are seven evil little bastards and seven little goodies. Then there's only one of me." She rolled her hips against Harley's.

"Thanks," Harley said as she twisted the door handle and slipped into her room, slamming the door behind her.

"Seven, and one maybe." Harley peeked through the curtain and looked at Lucius.

He stared right back at her and made a gun with his hand, cocking his thumb and firing it at her.

"You're first, asshat!"

Chapter Twenty-two

Shielding her eyes from the sun peeking through the slit in the curtains, Harley turned her face away.

"Just a few more minutes isn't too much to ask. Is it?" she said to no one in particular.

Pulling the pillow, she covered her head. How she'd made it through the night was beyond her. She fully expected Lucius and/or Allie to barge into her room at any moment. She supposed she was lucky. Perhaps they'd had their fun and were planning their next way to torment her. Allie was the oddball in the equation. Harley wondered what to make of her.

Harley made quick work of her morning routine, opting for a sponge bath after looking at the shower. She shuddered, thinking about the lone pubic hair in the tub. It was enough to gross her out for days. She'd rather suffer a cold dunking in a river than a warm shower with someone else's DNA.

Slinging her jacket on, she gave the room one more pass before pushing out into the blinding sunlight. In front of her door sat a motorcycle with a big fat red bow on the tank. A card sat in the center of the bow. Pulling it out, she slit the envelope open and read the card out loud.

"A peace offering for last night. I hope you'll forgive me. Allie."

She tossed the card on the ground and turned

and walked away from the motorcycle. She didn't want the strings that usually came with a gift. And this one probably had more than a few attached. She was focused was getting home and back to her family. After that, she'd figure things out.

Hitting the edge of the pavement, she looked back down the road to the café and considered having breakfast, but there was only one problem. The café was shuttered. The single stoplight hanging across the street was out, and the gas station was dilapidated and beyond functioning. The trees lining the street, covered with copious amounts of hanging green moss, badly needed trimming. How could she have not noticed even that minor detail?

"What the hell?"

Loping down the street, she stopped in front of the diner. Windows had been broken out, and plywood covered the inside, preventing any other obstacles from entering. The screen door she'd shouldered her way through just yesterday hung at an angle by one hinge. Walking around the corner, she spotted the cigarette machine and the picnic bench. She patted her pockets and pulled out the lone cigarette and the pack of matches. This was seriously screwed up.

Looking back at the motel, she noticed the same thing. The window blinds behind the neon sign were twisted, broken as if someone had put their hand in the middle and swished the blinds around, destroying the tangled mess. The neon sign hung on only one of its chains and looked like it hadn't functioned in years. The Rambler still sat in the parking lot, rust eating away at its exterior. Where was the pristine Escalade?

How could she have imagined everything?

There was only one thing she could do now. Run.

Passing the office of the motel, she stopped, rubbed dirt away from the glass, and peeked in, starving. She put her back to the door and elbowed the glass, shattering it enough to slip her hand through and open it. Spider webs acted like window coverings, and dust was the new accessory on everything. Turning the register book around, she moved her finger down the rows. Her name sat at the bottom, but it wasn't written in fresh ink.

Christ, this wasn't happening, she thought, walking around the counter and rummaging through the drawers. After she pulled hard on a stuck drawer, it fell to the floor and littered the carpet with a box of ammunition and a gun. Scared to pick it up, she looked around as if waiting for the manager to come running.

Dead silence.

She pulled a few more drawers open, only to find pencils, motel stationery, and key fobs.

Scooping up the gun and ammunition, she stuffed them into her backpack and then found a package of cookies, a couple of candy bars, and a dried-up apple on the desk behind the counter. She'd take what she could get. She definitely had eaten worse. The apple, though, was where she drew the line. She'd leave that for the ghost that haunted this place.

The curtain to the back apartment moved from the breeze coming in from the door.

Should she?

Maybe she'd find food back there?

Yeah, or maybe she'd find the manager and his wife's dead bodies.

Spooked, she bolted for the door. Something brushed her face as she slipped past the wavering curtain. Definitely time to go. Catching the door with her foot, she slammed it shut, shattering the glass.

"Send me a bill. Somehow I think you know where I live," she tossed over her shoulder to no one.

Racing back to the motorcycle still sitting in front of her room, she picked up the card, reread it, and made sure it didn't have Lucius's name on it. Giving the bike another look, she suddenly realized this was her bike. She walked a circle around it and recognized a scratch on the fender from a drummer walking in a Pride parade two years ago. Fingering the damaged spot, she remembered the day like it was yesterday. She was still pissed at the careless woman.

Pulling her backpack off, she stuffed it into the hard bag and pulled the helmet from the bitch seat. Inspecting it, she noted it too was her helmet. How considerate of Allie, she thought acerbically. She'd ponder all of this later. Her need to get back to her body and home to her mother was overwhelming. Checking her pack, she felt around for her keychain.

"God, please don't tell me I left my keys back at the campground. Please." She pleaded with the deity.

She fingered a set of metal and almost whooped it up when she extracted the set of keys. At least things were sort of going her way. Slipping the key in, she crossed her fingers as she cranked the temperamental monstrosity. Its low-throated groan as the battery pushed the engine made her smile.

"Come on, girl, turn over."

Rubbing the tank, she felt as if she were rubbing her cat's belly. Before she knew it, the engine gave up its protest and purred like the metal kitten Harley remembered.

"Nice." She revved the engine, cleaning out any metaphorical cobwebs that might have collected. Then she pulled the clutch, kicked it down into gear, and edged her way to the pavement. Like a horse running to the barn. She pointed the metal horse home and gunned it.

Easing into the corner, Harley leaned with her bike. The feeling of freedom when she rode her bike put her at ease. As she bent into the turn, exhilaration made her push her bike beyond its limits like a junkie mainlining heroin. Electricity coursed through her as she pulled on the throttle and passed a farm tractor crawling down the road.

A sign whizzed past her. She was more than a few miles from home. If she was a Paladin, was she in her territory? Before she could consider the topic further, a quick-moving black blur off to the left in front of her caught her attention. Eating up the pavement, she'd hit them in…

Four.

Should she swerve to avoid hitting the mass?

Three.

What was that huge mass made of?

Two.

She recognized the giant flock of Ravens too late to evade them. Even if she could, where would she go? Valley on the left and forest on the right. The kamikaze mass was aimed right for her. Beaks tore at her body, aimed for her head, and shrouded her view. Barely able to see the curve in front, she did her best to lean the bike.

It was no use. The birds were everywhere, sacrificing themselves to kill her. Harley let go of the throttle and put the bike down. If she was lucky she'd skid off the road, have some road rash, but she'd survive. She hoped. The birds flocked around her and the bike as it tumbled over and over.

Not exactly the crash she was hoping for. It was going to be brutal. The last thing Harley saw was her mother's face.

"It's all right, dear. You can go," her mother said, her voice somber.

Go? Where was she *going*?

Total blackness encased Harley. Resignation hit her and she relaxed, finally accepting her fate. It was over, at last.

Chapter Twenty-three

I s she dead? Please tell me she isn't dead."
"Calm down, Jack. Harley?"

Shit, she wasn't dead, but she wished she were. Her body was screaming in pain. Harley tried to move her hands to push herself up but couldn't.

Oh, God!

Tap, tap.

"Harley, can you hear me? Wake up. I know you're not dead," Dawn said. She gently pulled the helmet visor up and stared down into Harley's eyes. "Speak to me, damn it."

"Sit her up," Jack offered.

"No. Don't move me," Harley whispered.

"Are you okay?" Jack pushed his head down next to Dawn's.

"I can't move." Harley panicked.

"Oh, Christ. What were you doing on that thing? You could have been killed."

"Uhm, I don't think it was her fault. There are dead birds all over the bike, Dawn," Jack said, pulling one from the spokes by its wing and holding it up for inspection. The large, bloodied bird started shaking in Jack's grasp and then disappeared. A black fog floated in its place.

"Ouch, that stuff burns," Jack said, swishing his hand around.

"Get away from there, Jack," Dawn ordered him.

"This is Lucius's doing. Harley, where'd you get the bike?"

"Allie."

"Allie?" Dawn's brows and forehead furrowed. "As in my sister, Allie?"

Harley didn't say anything. She didn't have to. She knew Dawn read her mind.

"You have a sister? Who's Lucius?" Jack asked, pulling another bird from the spokes of the bike.

"Doesn't matter." Dawn hovered over the opening of the helmet. "Anything you want to tell me?"

Dawn sounded jealous. Harley would've laughed if she didn't hurt so bad. She could barely breathe and suspected she had a punctured lung. Worse, she pretty much figured her neck was broken, which was the reason she couldn't move.

The smell of gasoline, burnt rubber, dirt, and blood assaulted her senses. Wetness coated her back.

"Is that gas I smell?" Harley could feel it seeping up her back. This wasn't good. If an errant spark hit, they'd be toast. "I'm soaked, Dawn. You have to get out of here. I can't move, and if someone drives by and throws a cigarette out—or worse, if Lucius just happens to show up with that cigar of his—we're all dead."

"I'm not leaving you, so relax."

Dawn undid the chinstrap to the helmet and was going to pull it off when Harley stopped her.

"Don't. My neck is broken."

Dawn's hands trembled as she held Harley's hands. "I can fix you, but it's going to hurt like hell."

"What other options do I have? I'll die if you move me."

"I won't let you die. Trust me." Dawn's hand brushed along Harley's shoulder and squeezed it gently.

She looked around and studied her surroundings. "Jack, I need to you keep watch. Once I start, I won't be here, so I need you to be my eyes and ears in case someone comes around."

"What? Me? I can't do anything, remember?" He swished his hands through Dawn for effect.

"You can warn me of danger. I need you to protect us."

"Why? You're like a god or something. Who could hurt you?"

His whining was starting to grate on Harley. "Jesus, Jack, grow a pair. You want me to take you to your gate? I can't do that if I'm dead, so do what Dawn says and keep an eye out for anything suspicious." Harley huffed out the command. She was fading fast.

"You promise to take me to my gate, Harley?"

"Promise," she gasped, trying to suck in as much air as she could. Her head was flying higher than the clouds from lack of oxygen, and she could have sworn she saw a cloud shaped like a piece of cake floating by. Maybe that was a metaphor for what Dawn was about to do. "Piece of cake," she whispered, closing her eyes.

"I'm at my most vulnerable when I heal a Paladin. It's why we don't usually do it out in the open. Harley can't be moved and she's dying, Jack. Do you understand?" Dawn impaled him with her stare. She meant business.

Jack nodded. "Fine." Kicking the dirt, he sat down and crossed his legs, his back to them.

Dawn bent down and put her hands on Harley's barely moving chest. "I won't lie. This is going to hurt like a son-of-a-bitch. Scream if you want. Better yet…" She grabbed a good-sized twig, rubbed it on her pants, and broke it into a manageable piece. "Bite down on this."

"Why?"

"Trust me. You're going to need it."

Slipping it between Harley's lips, Dawn rested her hands above Harley's chest.

"*Medico. Auxilio. Emaculo.*" Dawn's hands started to glow as she touched Harley's body. She repeated, "*Medico. Auxilio. Emaculo. Medico. Auxilio. Emaculo.*"

As she moved her hands back and forth slowly, Harley slipped a glance at her. Her aura was wrapped around herself and Harley. Energy vibrated like a sound against Harley's chest. A slow build-up of warmth ebbed its way through Harley's body. Pain, like an ice pick, pushed through her joints, into her chest and heart.

She screamed.

Her broken bones ground against each other as they moved and reset. Her muscles were being pulled taut. Behind her eyelids, a fireworks display like nothing she'd ever seen before went off as her head exploded inside. Like a constrictor was wrapping around its victim, her head and body seized.

She was in agony.

"Stop. You're hurting her," Jack cried as he covered his ears. Harley wished she could comfort the poor soul, but he was making her even more anxious. She watched as he paced back and forth staring at her motionless body. Shaking his hands nervously, he begged again. "I can't listen to... You have to stop. You're hurting her. Please."

"Jack, back away. If you touch me, you'll cease to exist."

He stopped in the dirt path he'd carved out. "You

mean die?"

"Never to return. Please let me do my job."

"Oh, God, she looks like she's dead already."

"Stop," Dawn commanded. "Sit back down and watch for intruders."

Seconds, minutes, maybe hours passed, with Dawn's voice the only thing seeping into Harley's awareness.

"*Medico. Auxilio. Emaculo.*"

The water felt so warm. Embracing. Nurturing. Harley didn't want to leave this place. It spoke it her like a mother speaks to its child in the womb. A caress glided over her and then stroked her hair. Deep down inside her soul, she felt it calling her name.

"Come forward, child." A woman's soothing voice reached out like a hand and pulled Harley forward from the liquid. "Is it your time?"

Harley shielded her eyes as she peered up at the woman sitting on a bench. She couldn't see her face. The sun behind her wrapped around her silhouette and warmed Harley.

She wasn't sure of the question so she answered honestly. "I don't know."

"Paladin, do you know where you are?"

She shook her head.

The birthmark on Harley's chest exploded in light and etched itself on the woman's own chest. This is too weird, Harley thought, tracing the edges of the birthmark with her fingertips.

"This is your birthright, child." The woman did the same, tracing her own mark with her fingers.

"My birthright?"

"A great Paladin has been foretold for eons. She comes to balance out the life scales of justice." The woman tilted her head toward the mark, fingered it again, and then lifted her head. "Yours is not yet complete, Paladin. You are still needed in the other domain." The woman lifted her hand.

"But...wait...who are you?"

"Do you not recognize your own mother, child?"

"Mom?"

"I'm not your birth mother, but—"

A young girl sprinted up behind the woman and whispered in her ear. A palpable rage shot through the fluid they shared, knocking Harley backward.

"You must go back, Paladin. My daughter needs you. There will be many who will try to kill you, but you carry my mark." She touched her chest again. "You will be hunted. There are those who want to tilt the scales in their favor. Your death would aid them in their quest to take over this domain."

Harley nodded yet didn't understand a thing the woman was saying.

"You'll be tempted by those who present a false image, who offer strength and protection. But remember, there is only one Protector for each Paladin. Watch carefully and judge wisely."

The girl tugged on the shroud the woman wrapped tighter around herself. Nodding, she got up. "Go back. This isn't your time or your destiny, yet. You are the only Paladin capable of killing the evil that was set loose on the universe." The woman pulled her hand forward, and Harley was dragged before the woman. Her beauty was indescribable, but her eyes were sorrowful.

"Be safe, my child. We shall meet again." She placed a kiss on Harley's forehead and then vanished, taking the brightness with her. The darkness was pitch-black, draping around Harley like a blanket. She reached her hand out and watched it disappear into the inkiness.

What was happening?

Go back?

Go back where?

She couldn't see anything. She stuck her foot out tentatively to take a step, but nothing was there. She couldn't feel anything. No ground, no water, nothing.

"Hey, how am I supposed to go back?" she yelled. "What the hell is going on here?"

Without warning, her body arched and then curled into itself, pain wrapping around her.

"Oh, God. Help."

Chapter Twenty-four

Harley's eyes popped open and she gasped for air. Sucking in a lungful, she held it and realized the pain was gone. The cloud-covered sky was still above her, so she was on this side of the ground. That was good news. Dawn was above her, studying her. That was good, right?

"What happened?" Harley tried to sit up but was paralyzed.

"You died."

"No, I didn't. I was with some woman. She called herself my mother."

Harley's fingers tingled, like tiny pins shooting through the tips and then moving up to her palms. She felt just like they'd fallen asleep. Inching up her hands, to her forearms and then her biceps, the needles stabbed every inch of her skin.

"Oh…" Dawn's expression was barely readable, a road map of changing landscapes: sorrow, confusion, and now apprehension.

"Who is she?"

Her body felt like it was a pincushion for a voodoo priestess. Tiny pricks pushed her muscles, and the pain leeched out of every pore. Suddenly it was like a thread was being pulled through her stomach. She arched up and shrieked in agony.

Dawn's warm touch eased her back onto the ground, her hands massaging Harley's limbs as she chanted the same words over and over again. Softly at first and then easing into a full-blown growl, Dawn's controlled voice said the words one last time. "*Medico. Auxilio. Emaculo.*"

Silence purged any sound, and nothing moved for several moments.

Then Harley could hear Dawn panting above her. A few trickles of sweat rolled down her face. Collecting with others on the way down, they dropped to the dirt. Harley heard them hit with a slight thud.

Closing her eyes, she just wanted to rest, to think about what had just happened and wonder, why her?

Her fingers twitched, the pinpricks easing slightly. She moved her index finger and thumb back and forth, snapping them together. The noise seemed to echo enough that Dawn looked at Harley's hand.

"Do that again?" she commanded.

Harley slowly tapped them together. Her other fingers weren't so accommodating, were still stiff and unbending. "That's all I got."

Dawn smiled down at her. "It's a start and you're not dead."

"Lucky me. How come I wish I was right about now?" The helmet limited her view, but she tried to see Jack. "Is he okay?"

"He will be. I just told him that if he didn't shut up, I would banish him forever."

"Oh."

"Yeah, he kind of got on my nerves."

"Uh-huh."

Dawn hovered over Harley, touching her body. "Can you move anything else?"

"Who was that woman, Dawn?"

"Harley, I'd really like to sit here and chat, but

we're out here in the open, and you're not exactly able to protect Jack. So, please see if you can move anything else." Dawn picked up Harley's hand and turned it over. The kiss Dawn placed on her palm provided Harley with a jolt right to her loins.

"That's working," Harley said.

"What's working?"

"Never mind."

"Did you feel that?"

"Oh yeah, I felt that all right." Thank God the helmet covered most of her face, saving her the embarrassment of the blush crawling its way up her neck and checks.

"How's your head feeling?"

"No headache. That's a good sign, right?"

"I think so." Dawn didn't sound too convincing.

"What do you mean, you think so?"

"You died, Harley. So I'd say that the fact that you're even talking right now is a miracle. Wouldn't you?"

"But I didn't die. That's what I'm trying to tell you."

Dawn picked up Harley's hand and kissed it again. Rubbing the back of it against her face, she looked lovingly at Harley. Something passed between them, but Harley wasn't sure she wanted to put a name to the emotion. She wasn't ready for that, not yet.

"I need to get you out of the open and somewhere safe. Jack?"

"Yeah." He scurried to his feet, then dusted off his hands and clothes. "What's up?"

"We need to move Harley. It's going to take time for her to recover her ability to get around."

Hoisting Harley off the ground, Dawn ordered

Jack to the trees. "We'll be out of sight here."

"But what about—"

"We'll get you to your gate, Jack. Relax."

Harley felt a chill as they moved her under a tree. "My legs are cold. Is that a bad sign?"

Dawn and Jack looked at each other.

"You wet yourself," Dawn whispered.

"What? Are you kidding me?" If the rocks around her would offer a respite from the embarrassment she was feeling, she would crawl under one. "I have a spare pair of pants in my backpack. Can you get them? Please?"

"Harley, it's one of the effects of the healing process. It's nothing to be ashamed of." Dawn was trying to be upbeat. "It happens to everyone."

"Yeah, well, I'm wet, and Jack is standing right there. Can I have my pants, please? Wait? Let's try to get this helmet off my head."

"But—"

"But what? You said that you healed me. I want this damn helmet off, so let's see if I'm healed. Can't you just morph it off?"

"No. I can't morph inanimate objects. I can morph people but not make this disappear. I don't do magic, Harley." It was the way Dawn stressed the last syllable of her name and the cross look that gave Harley pause. Standing, Dawn started to go for Harley's pants but stopped. "Wait. Perhaps I can fracture the helmet?"

"What?" Fracturing the helmet sounded worse than just pulling it off her head.

"I can move things, like people, so—"

"Then why can't you just morph me out of the helmet?"

"Because you're in it. It would go with you."

"Oh."

Kneeling back down, Dawn put her hands on the helmet and concentrated. Harley felt the quick surge in temperature on her head and was just about to tell Dawn to stop when Dawn yelled.

"I did it. I busted the helmet."

Harley could hear as Dawn started pulling at pieces of the helmet, twisting her neck slightly. Panicked, she said, "Hey, you're moving my head and my neck. Is that okay?"

"Oh, sorry," Dawn said, stopping.

"Don't stop. I'm still here so that's a good thing."

"Jack, pull Harley's knife from her pocket and see if you can cut away the liner."

"Really?" Jack asked, reaching for the knife and demonstrating he wasn't going to be able to comply with her command.

"Oh yeah, sorry." Dawn reached for it herself. Palming the knife, she flicked it open with a flick of her wrist, slowly and gently slicing off the last pieces of the liner.

"There." Dawn sat back on her heels, crossed her arms, and smiled.

Glad to be free of the helmet, Harley looked around her world with renewed interest. She never wanted to put a helmet on again. Well, okay, just not anytime soon. Slowly she turned her head to the side and smiled at Dawn.

"Thanks."

"My pleasure.'

"You saved my life. I owe you. You didn't have to do that." Harley tried to move her hand to reach for Dawn but was barely able to move her fingers. "I'm sorry about the other day. I...I just didn't think I was ready to handle the mantle of a Paladin. I shouldn't have said those things to you, especially not after that wonderful night. I'm an ass. I won't deny that I'm pretty good at putting both my feet in my mouth."

Dawn's fingers traced the veins protruding from the back of Harley's hand. She wouldn't look at Harley as she spoke. "Words have power, can produce pain, and should be considered wisely before being spoken."

"I know. I wouldn't blame you if you didn't accept my apology. It's just that I've never faced this type of situation. I mean, I've never been a Paladin before."

Dawn looked at Harley with a dubious expression.

"Okay, well, in this lifetime, I mean. I might have been something in past lives, but I have nothing to compare it to here. I can't remember everything yet. It's coming back to me like photographs I just found in a dusty album." It took everything Harley had to push her hand over and grab Dawn's hand. "I'm sorry."

"I understand. We've been through this before, and it never gets easier."

"I've hurt you before, haven't I?" Harley hated to admit it, but she knew it was true. "I guess I don't get better with age, do I?"

"You do. You do." Dawn lifted Harley's palm to her lips and dusted it with a kiss.

"Who was the woman?"

They locked gazes and Dawn's didn't falter. Harley felt as if she was searching for something to say.

"We had the same birthmark or scar. It lit up and…"

"Let me look." Dawn pulled Harley's shirt back and studied the symbol. Another mark had been added to the symbol.

"What's wrong?"

"Did it hurt?"

"Did what hurt?"

"The new moon line added to your birthmark."

"What? What are you talking about?" Harley peered down at her scar and noticed the red arc that was attached to the symbol. "What the hell is that?"

"Mother's given you another rank." Dawn ran her finger over the red half-moon. "You've risen to the next level in Paladins, Harley."

"How is that possible?"

"I don't know. Something's happened recently." Dawn pushed away from Harley. "We need to get you some food and make you comfortable. We can talk about all this later."

"Okay."

Harley could feel uneasiness in Dawn, so she didn't push it. They had time. She hoped.

"Now can I have my pants?" she reminded Dawn. "I'd really like to get out of these wet ones, but I'll need your help."

"You want me to change you in front of Jack?"

"No. I want Jack to turn his back while you help me change my pants," Harley suggested.

Jack pointed deeper into the trees. "I'll just be over there."

"Do I need to remind you not to go too far?"

"Nope."

"Good."

Dawn came back with Harley's pants swinging from her hand. Hopefully the healing was complete and Harley could move without issue. Otherwise Dawn would have to wait a few more minutes before torturing Harley's body by putting on a dry pair of pants.

Leaning up against a tree, she could scan the whole area. Dawn and Jack were resting close enough that, if they had unexpected visitors, they wouldn't be seen.

"Anything I should know about your meeting with my sister Alleo?"

Harley realized they had a lot to talk about, but this wasn't where she would have started. She wanted to know about being dropped into that vacant town miles back. Why would Dawn do that to her? Sure, she'd been wishy-washy about being a Paladin, but wasn't everyone who had that much responsibility thrust on them? Most people didn't want to save the world. Did they? Now, aware that not only was she a Paladin—which she never wanted in the first place—but that she was moving up in their ranks, Harley had even more to deal with. She owed Dawn her life, but somehow, she was also responsible to her destiny. So going home and back to her regular life was out of the question, for now.

Something niggled at the back of her brain, like a distant memory that she just couldn't grasp but was sure was of utmost importance. She needed to get Jack to his gate. Right away. She wasn't certain how she knew, but something told her Jack had only a small window of time during which to cross over. A biting cold ran through her bones.

"Can you help me up?" she asked Dawn.

"What's wrong?"

She didn't want to tell Dawn that she had a feeling danger was coming. Dawn could probably feel it, too.

"I want to see if I can walk yet."

Dawn reached down and Harley grabbed her forearms. Dawn leaned back as Harley scooted her way up the trunk of the tree. As she inched higher, her heart raced and her head seemed to float. Dawn's arms immediately went around Harley's waist to steady her. Their bodies touched, breast against breast, loins against loins. Harley's breath mingled with Dawn's as she turned her face. She didn't resist the urge to kiss Dawn.

Soft pliant lips pressed against hers. "I'm the anchor that keeps you in this world, aren't I?"

"What do you mean?" Dawn kissed Harley again, this time with more passion.

"You—" Another kiss to shut her up. "Would you be with your *mother* if it wasn't for me—" Another kiss. "I know." Another kiss, this one lingering before she finally broke it off and said, "I can feel it."

Dawn pulled back but didn't let Harley go. "No. I'm right where I'm supposed to be, Harley. I'm your Protector. It's my job."

"Good to know that I'm just a job." Harley tried to break free from Dawn's grip, but Dawn held her tighter.

"I didn't mean it that way. You're not a job. You're my—"

The air vibrated with a sonic shock, almost knocking the three of them off their feet. A dark-clad figure walked out of the middle of the glowing mass that was imploding behind her with the wave, energy oozing from her like bad perfume on a hot day. The way she sauntered closer, Harley recognized who it was immediately. Allie was walking sex, and she knew it.

Jack sucked in a breath, obviously realizing this was a woman. His heart was beating out a tempo so fast that, if he hadn't already been dead, he would have most likely have keeled over any minute from a heart attack.

Dawn, on the other hand, was ice-cold, her purple aura frozen over in a split second and replaced by a blackish-blue one. Her hands on her hips, she just stared at Allie. God, Harley was glad she wasn't on the receiving end of that look. It would wither a healthy tree down to a burnt-out sapling.

"What are you doing here, Alleo?"

"Sister, is that any way to greet your long-lost sibling?" Allie smiled and ran a finger over Jack's chest. "And who are you, stud?"

Suddenly the cat had Jack's overused tongue. Harley cocked her head at Jack and pursed her lips. Of course, he was a male, and Allie was a giant black hole of sexy. Allie ran her fingers through Jack's short hair and then around the hole in his chest.

"What happened here?"

No one answered.

"Did I interrupt something?" Allie swung her leather-clad hips from side to side, walking around the motorcycle, studying the broken machine. Picking up a dead Raven, she held it closer for inspection. Like a quality-assurance analyst, she tossed it to the side without another look. "Oh, I see you've had an accident."

Pointing toward the group, she flicked a ruby-tipped fingernail at Harley and then seductively slipped it between her lips covered in the matching lipstick. She skimmed the tip of it with her tongue and then tossed a wicked smile at Harley.

Harley was going to combust right there if she didn't get herself together.

"Harley, right?" Allie smiled. Her teeth were almost as blinding as Lucius's.

It must be an evil-deity thing, Harley thought.

"I'll ask again. What are you doing here, Alleo? Don't tell me you just happened to be in the neighborhood." Dawn stood between the group and her sister.

Protective or jealous? Harley wondered.

"Neither," Dawn said over her shoulder to Harley.

"You look good, Sister. It's been way too long." Allie stopped her peacock walk and stood facing Dawn, hands on her hips. She was the polar opposite of her sister. Her aura was flaming red and bounced around her like she was on fire. The silhouette of Allie inside the aura was breathtaking. Her energy was magnetic, and Harley was having a hard time focusing on anything else. Funny, she hadn't been like this last night when Lucius was around and her aura was royal blue. She didn't know what all the colors meant yet, but she'd learn. You didn't need to be a spiritualist to know black was negative, white was purity, and red... well, red was fire-hot.

Allie raised her palms toward Harley. "You're injured. Perhaps I can help?"

A smooth kinetic fluidity passed between them, and unfortunately, her body responded immediately. Harley closed her eyes and embraced the touching. Bad idea on her part, as Dawn pierced her with a gaze similar to the one she'd flashed at Allie. Harley didn't have to open her eyes to see it, but Jack's sudden intake of breath and the heat from Dawn told her that it was bad news.

"We don't need your help, Alleo. She's fine."

Dawn put herself between her sister and Harley.

If this had been another time and place, say a gay bar, Harley would laugh at the back-and-forth banter between the two women. Except this wasn't that place, and Allie wasn't just a woman flirting with her. She was flirting, right?

"I'm fine. Thanks for asking."

"I see you got my little gift," she said, pointing to the crumpled mess.

"Yes. I was a little surprised to find it waiting outside my motel room."

"Good surprise, I hope," Allie purred.

All eyes were on Harley, waiting for her to respond.

Chapter Twenty-five

Great. The only thing missing was Lucius. Harley searched the sky, waiting for him to drop out of it any moment.

"Oh, don't worry. My little brother is coming." Allie winked at Harley.

God, she wished Allie wouldn't do that in front of Dawn. Dawn would get all the wrong ideas. But then again, Harley suspected Allie often liked to take Dawn's toys and play with them. It was a sibling thing. She'd seen her cousins do it all the time. Establish ownership, or territory, and then take it away, or in Lucius's case, piss all over it like a dog.

"You don't look so good. Perhaps I can help." Allie was in Harley's space in an instant, completely maneuvering around Dawn before anyone could blink.

Harley was never going to get used to the things Protectors could do, assuming Allie was a Protector, or at least a dark Protector. Neither role had been established clearly enough for Harley's liking, and she hadn't had time to discuss all of this with Dawn. Heck, they hadn't even talked about how Dawn had abandoned her the day before. She would just add this to the long list of questions she was compiling in her head.

"You were with both Lucius *and* Allie last night?" It was more of a statement than a question, but the intent was clear. Harley had screwed up somehow.

"Not to worry. I was protecting your precious Paladin." Allie toyed with a piece of Harley's hair. "It was Lucius I was worried about, Sister."

Harley felt like she was caught in a trap with no way out. Jack was surprisingly silent so she looked over at him. Something between fear and lust was etched across his face.

Harley poked him in the ribs. "Jack, wipe your mouth. You're drooling."

"You're in deep shit here, buddy."

"Tell me about it."

"You should be thanking me, Sister. Our brother had your Paladin in a hex, and she didn't look like she was going to make it out alive." Allie stalked her sister, cutting a circle around her big enough to avoid the darkening aura. "He took her back to her mother's death, made her relive it."

Harley froze as the memory played again in her head. The woman lying in her arms, begging Harley to find her brothers and kill Lucius. Her anger sparked again, and she remembered the vow she'd made in her room.

Kill him.

Kill all the evil ones.

"Something's different about you this morning, Paladin. What is it?" Allie smiled. Her eyes narrowed and focused on Harley's face, and then she cruised Harley's body. Her gaze stopped at Harley's chest— more specifically, where her birthmark was and its new moon line.

"You've seen Mother."

The way Allie said it, with such reverence, surprised Harley.

"You've been given your moon line. Well, that's

an interesting twist of events."

"Why?" Harley asked.

Allie turned to Dawn. "You haven't told her?"

Dawn only pursed her lips and raised an eyebrow. Something was definitely going on between these sisters.

"She hasn't told you what the moon line means?"

"No."

"Can I tell her, Sister dear?"

"We don't have time for chitchat, Alleo." Dawn sneered at her sister and then stood between Harley and Allie.

"You see, Paladin. Each mark on your tattoo, what you call your birthmark, is given for a battle won, a path taken that saves a life, achieving a higher level of consciousness, or an evil Protector killed." Allie put her palm toward Harley's chest, closed her eyes, and then squeezed her hand closed. "Your birthmark, tattoo, whatever you're calling it, isn't an accident. You carry it through each life, assuming you aren't killed by a Protector, accidentally, of course."

"She knows all this, Sister."

"Actually, you never said anything about new lines being added."

"About the new power you'll get with the new line?"

"Nope." Harley glanced sideways at Dawn, who shot her a cross look. What else was she keeping from her? Granted, they'd only recently met. Well, and had sex, but Dawn could have filled her in on a few more details then, yet she hadn't explained any of this when Harley had gone a little cray-cray. Maybe a few more details would have smoothed things over for her. Maybe she wouldn't have busted a seam, now that she thought about it.

"I didn't have a chance to tell you everything. I figured once Jack got to his gate, we'd have time then."

"Well, I mean I knew about the mark—"

"Not just a mark. The mark of a Paladin. We all have them." Allie pulled her leather jacket aside and flashed her intricate design. Like Dawn's, it was detailed and almost identical, except Dawn's was a different color, almost white. In fact, now that Harley thought about it, she'd only seen it when Dawn's aura changed during sex. It had been so fast, Harley had assumed she'd imagined it.

"Well, yours isn't *just* like ours. You see, ours is for service to a god or goddess, and then when they were all eliminated, we were granted Protector status. Sister here was handmaiden to Aphrodite. I, handmaiden to Apollo, hence my penchant for storms. I'm otherwise known as the storm goddess."

Allie whirled her hands around and whipped the winds into a cyclone. Leaves, dirt, and a few dead birds swirled around before she dropped her hand and let it die.

"Wait. What do you mean, the gods were eliminated?"

"Oh, hmm. Something for another era when we all get together for story time."

"You mean the Gathering?" Harley was confused. Gods dying, handmaidens, nothing made sense.

"Oh, so you do know about the Gathering. Has Mother called one and I wasn't told?"

Dawn and Harley answered in unison. "No."

"Ah, good. I'd hate to miss a Gathering."

"You aren't invited. Remember?" Dawn said.

"Details, details."

"Why aren't you invited?"

"We don't have time for this. Harley, pick up your things. If you're strong enough, we need to get Jack to his gate." Dawn pulled Harley along and grabbed Jack by the hand. "Unless you'd like to come along, Sister," Dawn offered.

Allie blanched at the suggestion. "I'm good, thanks. I have things that need my attention."

"I'm sure you do."

"I'm sure I'll be seeing you again, Harley. Right?"

"I don't think that's a good idea." Harley went cold. "I'm sure you heard what I said to Lucius last night."

"I did."

"So, you never said if you were like him or not."

"No, I guess I didn't, did I?" Allie pressed a crimson tip to her lips. "I haven't decided which team I like to play for, so I guess that means I'm a free agent."

Harley turned to Dawn. "Can she do that?"

"What did you say to Lucius, Harley?"

Harley turned and picked up her things. She flexed her legs. She was smart enough to know it was time to get out of this Greek drama. Limping away, she pulled Jack with her and left Dawn behind.

"What did she say to Lucius, Alleo?"

Allie flung her hand up and was gone, leaving Dawn to trail after Harley. "What did you say to Lucius last night, Harley?"

Chapter Twenty-six

Harley ignored the questions being tossed behind her. If Dawn didn't have to tell her what the hell was going on, neither did she. Screw it. She'd get Jack to his gate, then find someone to tell her about the moon line and the rest of her tattoo. What new power had she acquired?

Maybe it's the cloak of invisibility? She laughed. At least she still had her sense of humor. For now.

Jack piped up. "What are you laughing at?"

"Nothing. Okay, Jack, I want you to think about where your gate might be. We don't have a lot of time here."

"No kidding."

Harley kept walking. "Animal, vegetable, mineral?"

"What?"

"I don't know. Did you play that guessing game when you were a kid?"

"Sure, but what does that have to do with getting me to my gate?"

"I'm trying to stimulate my mind as much as I'm trying to stimulate yours, Jack."

"God, you still don't know how to get me to my gate?"

Harley concentrated. She could chew gum and walk, so she could surely walk and concentrate, too.

"Your gate is in my territory. Have you always

lived here?"

There had to be a connection between Jack's life and Harley's. She just had to figure it out. Dawn said Paladins had territory. Jack's gate had to be within those boundaries, obviously.

"Jack, what three things do you do consistently?"

"You mean other than shower, eat, and go to the bathroom?"

"Funny. What do you like to do that you could do every day if you were allowed to?"

Jack looked at her strangely before responding. "I'm a guy. Really?"

"Geez, Jack. Help me out here, buddy."

"I don't know, Harley. Work, I guess. Ever since my mom died, my dad's been depending on me to help out. Now he's got the early stage of dementia, so it's tough. I miss my mom and I—"

"Stop." Something struck Harley. Was his mom the key? Everyone had someone, or some place, they had a deep connection to – girlfriend, dog, lover, childhood home – someone or something that they connected to their whole life. At least that's how it was for her. The dream earlier of her parents flashed. "Your mom's dead?"

"Yeah. Why?"

"When, how, where? Wait. I mean how old were you when she died?"

Jack choked back tears. "God, Harley. Really? This is hard enough without having to relive that time in my life."

Harley put her arm around Jack's shoulders. "I'm sorry. I know how difficult this is for you."

"How? Your mom isn't dead."

Harley remembered last night's events, courtesy

of Lucius. She, too, choked back a sob. It was so fresh, just like she'd been there, again.

"This isn't my first rodeo, remember?" Harley patted him on the back. "When did your mom die?"

"When I was eight."

"Wow."

"Where was your favorite place to go with her?"

"What? I don't know."

"Think, Jack. Okay. Where did she die?"

His once-boyish looks morphed into a look Harley was familiar with, one she'd seen a dozen times. Grief was an emotion like no other. Pain and denial etched their way across Jack's face. He hesitated, his mouth moving but nothing coming out.

"Jack?"

"She was so young, so vibrant. I miss her every day, Harley." Jack, who took to theatrics easily, started to bawl. Only this wasn't a temper tantrum. This was a child grieving for his lost mother. The pain never went away. It only buried deeper in the recesses of the soul, coming out at the worst time. Harley had dug up this pain, and now she'd have to wait until Jack was ready to talk about it. Only they didn't have that kind of time.

"I'm sorry, Jack. I know this is hard, but I think this might be the way back to your gate."

"What do you mean?"

"I don't know. I just have a feeling." Harley clasped her hand around his and hugged his shoulders. "Where did she die? You don't have to tell me about the circumstances, just where."

Jack wiped at the snot dripping from his nose and sucked in a short sob. "My dad murdered her. She was going to leave him, and he…"

Harley closed her eyes and shivered. Someone

had just walked across her own grave.

"I'm so sorry, Jack."

Her anger was building as she was reminded once again about Lucius and his dirty deed. She wasn't about to forget her promise last night. He would die in this lifetime. She would see to it.

Jack ran his nose down the length of his shirt. "Why? You didn't do it."

"No, but I've seen my own mother murdered in front of me, and I know how that feels."

"God, Harley. I'm sorry. I didn't know."

Harley slapped him on the shoulder and then gave it a buddy squeeze. "It's okay."

She gave him a few minutes to compose himself before she asked her next question.

"What happened to your father?"

"He's in prison for the rest of his life."

"Brothers, sisters?"

"Yeah, two of each."

"Any of them passed on?"

He shook his head and looked off at nothing in particular.

"Okay, well, once again…did you and your mom have a particular place you liked to spend time?"

"The park by my house."

"That's where we'll start."

"The park?"

"If that was where you were happy, it makes sense that your gate might be there."

"Really, that almost seems too obvious, Harley."

"Sometimes the simplest answers are the right answers. Besides, you're not there yet. We have to get you to the playground. Lucius isn't going to make it that easy on me."

"Who is this Lucius guy?"

"He's Dawn's brother and he's pure evil." Harley stood and pulled her backpack on. "Oh, and he either wants me to join his team or die. My choice."

"He's the one who's been sending the birds and Dark Souls, isn't he? It hasn't been a coincidence, has it?"

"No."

"What about Alleo? Is she on our side or his?"

Harley stalked off.

That has yet to be seen.

Chapter Twenty-seven

Jack, I need to stop and rest." Harley bent over and gasped. "Over there by those rocks. They should give us enough cover for me to catch my breath."

"Harley…" Jack whined, as usual.

"Just a few hours ago, every bone in my body was broken."

"Not every bone."

Dawn sided with Harley. "We can rest for a little while. Harley needs to get her strength back."

"Fine, but I need to stretch my legs. I don't think I can just sit around."

"Don't leave the area, Jack. Dark Souls are looking for you."

"Oh, right. Okay, how about I just sit over here?" He pointed to an outcropping of rocks.

"Fine," Harley said.

She thought about how they bantered back and forth like brother and sister. She'd never had a sibling and now knew what it felt like to constantly be challenged. She smiled internally, forced to admit that she liked it.

Harley pulled her gun from her belt and checked the clip. She needed to reload it. Chances were high that before she got Jack safely to his gate, they'd have to fight their way to it. Lucius wasn't about to give up, not this time. Not now that he knew Harley was alive in this life. They were headed for a showdown. Not the O.K. Corral type, but more like the fire-and-brimstone, come-to-Jesus moment everyone had at least once in a lifetime. Well, this was Lucius's last lifetime if she had anything to do with it. Why would Mother allow him to do the things he did? Did she know about his killing of Paladins? Of his evil deeds? Or was she an indulgent mother, like hers?

Dawn stood close to Harley, probably probing her mind. Served her right if she got messy jumping into Harley's head. It was chaos inside that dome. If Dawn was still here, Harley figured she might as well take advantage of it. Time to ask some questions.

"If you knew Jack was on borrowed time, why did you dump me like a guppy into that lake and bolt?"

"When a Paladin refuses their duty, there's a backup."

"Oh, an heir and a spare?"

"Yep, only yours is dead."

"What?"

"I went to find him, and he died the night I dumped you in the lake to cool off."

"How? Like murdered dead or just dead-'cause-it-was-his-time dead?"

"Murdered."

Harley winced. A chill crossed her body. "How?"

"Don't know, and I don't have time to find out. Jack's got to get to his gate tomorrow, or he walks this earth for eternity."

"Great. I don't want to have to run into him every time I'm taking another soul to their gate."

"You won't. He'll join the invisible ones, those destined to walk the earth and not be seen. It's a fate worse than eternal death. He'll be in limbo, forever."

"Forever?"

"Depends. Once a year, Paladins can pick a soul to cross back over. They're called *the chosen*. They have to attend to the Paladin for a year before they are allowed to go back. They risk being killed during that time, never to return, or they can choose to stay an invisible soul. Once the choice is made, it's final."

"God, aren't there enough rules and stuff that I have to remember? Now the pressure to get Jack to his gate is even greater."

"It is your duty. No more, no less. Every soul is a responsibility, a weight you carry for a lifetime."

Dawn put her hand on Harley's arm and a calm settled on them both. Well, for Harley it was more of a heightened sense of...sexual attraction to Dawn. Taking a deep breath, Harley tried to center herself. She wasn't up for a romp around the...where were they? She closed her eyes and rubbed her palms in a circular motion. She had so many questions, but time was the enemy at the moment.

"How do I narrow down where Jack's gate is?"

"It isn't a guessing game, I'll tell you that, but you know. Deep down inside, you know."

"If I knew I wouldn't be playing twenty questions with you. I'd be out hunting down Lucius and killing that bastard."

Harley slapped her hand across her mouth. Shit, if she could take those words back she would. Damn her quick-fire temper.

Dawn stood with her mouth agape. "Is that what you told Lucius? You told him you'd kill him? Harley..."

Harley held up her hand, stopping Dawn from continuing. "Don't, Dawn. He killed my mother. I watched him do it," Harley said through clenched teeth. Her jaw worked back and forth, and she ground her foot into the dirt. "He did it right in front of me. She begged for her life, Dawn. He stood there and dared me to stop him."

Harley dropped to her knees, stretching her arms out like she was still cradling her mother's body. Tears poured down her face in tribute to the woman who, so many centuries before, had begged her to kill Lucius. Who had given Harley life. A simple woman who'd given sons to the war and a daughter that she thought would be spared from a hard life of battle.

"Lucius mocked me last night, and he did it back then, too." She raised her tear-stained face to Dawn and reminded her. "You were there as well. You stopped me from killing him."

Harley thrust her hand up as if she were holding the sword that had delivered the jagged scar Lucius wore today, but she had also been ready to take his life that night. It was Dawn who'd stopped her, saved her brother from a Paladin's blade. Perhaps she should be furious with Dawn instead?

"You're the one that saved your brother that night, Dawn. You saw what he did to my family, yet you saved his life. Why?"

"Is your memory so incomplete that you don't remember that it was *you* who had to take your mother to her gate? Would you have wished her to be one of the invisible souls so you could exact your revenge?"

Harley hung her head, her shoulder slumped forward as she wept.

"Every Paladin is given the honor of escorting their family to their gate. It's the one last time they get to be with that soul before they must say good-bye.

Would you cheat your mother of that good-bye?"

Her hands at her face, Harley wept like she'd never wept before, the emotions of that memory flooding back. "I would have taken her after I killed Lucius. I promised her that night that I would kill him, and obviously I've failed in every life since."

Dawn knelt next to Harley and ran her fingers through the tangled locks. "You haven't failed. You've done extraordinary work in every lifetime, Harley."

"You stopped me from my duty to my family."

"I'm sorry. Would you feel better if you knew that in some lifetimes your path and Lucius's never crossed?"

"Not particularly, no." Harley wiped at her eyes. "He'll go after my mother this time around. I know it. I can feel it. He's here to taunt me, and I won't let him. I plan to keep that promise to my mother. He won't have her this time."

"Harley—"

"Don't try to stop me, Dawn. I made a vow to kill every evil out there, so don't get in the way."

"Or what? You'll kill me?"

Harley couldn't look at Dawn. She'd never kill Dawn, but she didn't know what Dawn would do to protect *her* family. While it didn't live up to Harley's idea of a family, Dawn was at a whole different level. Dead gods and goddesses, a mother who was aloof, and siblings that killed so they could rule the heavens and earth and whatever lay between them.

"I would never hurt you. You know that, so why even ask?"

A heavy heart hung between them. One knew her mission—kill Lucius—while the other worried about the soul and the journey it was about to take.

Chapter Twenty-eight

How much farther?" Jack whined yet again. Harley turned toward Dawn. "Can't you just morph us closer? I know you don't want to drop us in the middle of the park, but at least put us close enough to scout it out."

Dawn put her hand on Harley's arm. She wanted to say something. Harley could feel it. She had that *look*.

"We can talk after I get Jack to his gate. I promise. Please help me. I don't want Jack to be an invisible soul. It would crush me to know that my first soul was lost because of my stupidity."

"I'm worried your body isn't ready for the jump, Harley."

"Screw it. I'll take my chances. I've wasted too much trying to avoid being a Paladin. I need to woman up and accept my responsibilities."

Dawn offered her a half-smile and then nodded. "Jack, come over here."

"We're wasting time. I need to get to my gate. I'm starting to feel strange."

Harley and Dawn stared at Jack and then back at each other. Dawn grabbed their hands, completing the circle. She lowered her head, and within seconds her aura exploded.

☙ ☙ ☙ ☙

"Argh—" Dawn slapped her hand over Harley's mouth as she writhed in pain. Dawn was right. Harley hadn't been in any condition to jump. She was in agony. Curling into herself, she didn't move, fearing that any motion would cause more jolts of pain.

"Don't move. Listen to my voice, Paladin. You've received your moon line. You are at the next level of Paladin. Your mind is able to move beyond suffering, pain, and agony. Focus at a higher level. Embrace the pain, relax into it, and heal it."

Harley fixed her thoughts on every word Dawn was speaking.

A rush of blue light infused her body. Her head felt like it was floating. She touched the areas on her body that were in pain, healing each one. She placed her hands on either side of her head and concentrated. Warmth bounced between her palms. Pulling her hands down, she studied them. She'd only seen Dawn heal someone, but how was she…was that the new power Allie had spoken of?

"Harley, are you okay?" Jack slid down next to her prone body. "Harley, I'm feeling funny."

Looking at Jack, she could see he was starting to become transparent.

"Shit," she said, sitting up. "Let's get you to your gate, Jack."

Cautiously, the three of them moved in the trees surrounding the playground, if that's what one could call the decrepit eyesore. It had seen better days—no, decades—and this one was not one. Fingers of fog were starting to devour the playground, weaving in between the ladders, rings, and bars that in its heyday had held laughing children.

"Harley." Jack pulled her arm and pointed to

a person sitting on the broken and tilted merry-go-round, his or her back to them.

"Shit. It's probably Lucius. How did he know where we went?" She looked over at her Protector. "Dawn?"

She held up her hands. "Not me. I'm not open for a reading."

"I certainly didn't transmit this," Harley said defensively.

Both of them looked at Jack. "Hey, I don't even know this Lucius guy. So it wasn't me."

"I'm going to circle around and see if I can get a better look at our mystery guest," Harley whispered. She didn't know why. If it was Lucius, he'd be able to hear her from a mile away. She guessed that was his superpower.

"But what about me?"

"Jack, as soon as I know what we're dealing with, we can search out your gate. Keep your eyes open. It might magically appear. If it does, make a dash for it. I'll cover you."

"Are you sure?" He sounded as skeptical as she felt. No, she wasn't sure, but if it kept his eyes peeled for anything moving, he might just find something or someone.

"I'm sure. Dawn, watch him."

"Since when do I take orders from you, Paladin?"

"Sorry." Harley left it at that as she weaved between the unkempt overgrowth toward her target. If she was lucky, it was Lucius and she'd kill him on the spot. Problem solved. If it wasn't Lucius, then she'd deal with whomever it was and search for Jack's gate.

As she moved closer, she could hear a woman's cries. Odd. Who would be out here in this broken-down schoolyard, crying? Harley looked around to see if she could find the source. As she moved closer to the woman, the sobs became a bit louder.

Cautiously, she peered around the area before walking toward the woman. As Harley neared, the woman looked up, and Harley sucked in a breath. The woman was an exact replica of Jack but with one exception. Her face had the telltale signs of abuse: a black eye, bruised face, and a nose that had been broken several times.

"Hello?" she said, wiping her eyes.

"Hello. Are you Jack's mother?"

The woman didn't say anything, which frightened Harley. Had she been set up? Was this woman a decoy to lure them in and kill Jack? She spun around and ran toward her friends.

"Wait, yes. Yes, I'm Jack's mom."

Harley disregarded the words as she ran back fast to her companions. "Jack?"

"I'm right here. Who is it, Harley?"

Dawn met Harley's gaze and briefly nodded in confirmation. It was Jack's mom. How easy had that been?

Too easy.

"How is that possible?" Harley asked Dawn.

"It happens. Husbands wait for wives, parents wait for children. Or she could be an invisible soul."

"But we can see her," Harley said, pointing to the woman.

"What? Who is it, Harley?" Jack asked again.

"It's your mother, Jack."

"Wait. What? She's dead."

"I know. I think it's a trick." Harley confirmed what Jack was apparently thinking.

Chapter Twenty-nine

Minutes passed as the three of them watched the woman. She didn't move, only sat and cried. Harley had revealed her hand when she asked if the woman was Jack's mother. So why didn't she follow Harley?

"How do you know if she's my mother?"

"She looks just like you, Jack."

"Then I want to see her."

"Jack." Harley grabbed his arm, stopping him. "We need to be sure this isn't a trap."

"If that's my mom, Harley, I need to see her."

"I should warn you, she looks a little beat up. So prepare yourself."

"It's because that bastard beat her to death. That's how she died." Jack snarled.

"Okay, let's be logical about this, Jack. Suppose it is your mom. How did she get here?"

"I don't know. Ask *her*," he said, pointing to Dawn.

"My guess, if it's not a trap, is that she's been waiting for you, Jack."

"Why here? Why didn't she just come to me when I was alive?"

"What's that?" Harley asked, pointing to a wavering spot in the distance. To Harley it looked like one of those mirages in the desert. Heat radiating up created something that resembled a pond, but this mirage was more like a vibrating door, of sorts.

No one moved.

"It's Jack's gate," Dawn said.

They looked at the gate and back at Jack's mother, and then back at the gate.

"What do I do?" Jack was being pulled in two directions. His mother sat on the other side of the playground, while his gate was directly across from them and her. The distance was equal and equally deadly.

The hair on Harley's neck stood up. "Someone's here. I'm guessing a gatekeeper and his minions."

Dawn put her hand on Harley's arm, stopping her from moving. "You're protecting us, so don't go off half-cocked. Jack's going to need to make a decision."

"Can't we get him to his mother? I mean, jeez, she's been waiting for decades."

Jack was getting more transparent by the minute. "Please," he implored.

"Okay, but we need to be fast."

"Thank you." He started to run to his mom, but Harley stopped him.

Another person suddenly stood next to his mom. Her angular curves couldn't hide that it was Allie. She casually leaned against one of the handrails, and it looked like she was chatting with Jack's mom.

Harley shook her head. Could things get any worse? Don't answer that, she told herself. Lucius was suspiciously absent, and that didn't seem to be like him.

Allie strutted toward them, the fog parting like a crowd letting in a prize fighter. She was dressed in her uniform of choice—tight leather pants, boots—but she'd replaced her jacket with a sheer camisole, and her headlights were flashing.

She is definitely stepping up her game, Harley thought.

"Hello, Sister. I see you've found your gate, Jack." Allie smiled at the young man.

"How did you know we'd be here?" Dawn asked, her tone demanding.

"I recognized your young man here. He looks just like his mother."

"Why is she here? Where is her Paladin?"

"She is amongst the ranks of the invisible."

"What do you mean, she's invisible? I can see her right there," Jack said, loud enough that the woman turned and looked at them as they stood at the opposite end of the playground. "Mom." He waved his arms. "I'm coming."

"Where is her Paladin?" Dawn asked again. "You know the rules. Her Paladin can select her for another chance to cross over."

"He died protecting her."

"What? Who killed the Paladin?"

Allie looked at the woman sitting and then back at Jack. "Why don't you say hello to your mother, Jack?"

He ran, then scooped her up in his arms and twirled her around.

Harley persisted. "Who killed her Paladin?"

Allie still didn't say anything, as she seemed fixated on the touching family reunion playing out across the field. Harley jerked her around to face them.

"What happened?"

"Lucius killed her Paladin."

"What? Why?"

"Oh, you know how Lucius can be." She flung

her hand around. "I said something that pissed him off, and well…the Paladin paid the price."

"Does Mother know?"

"God, no. It wasn't that big of a deal." Allie pursed her lips, hugged herself, and turned her attention back to Harley. "So, how are you feeling?"

Harley didn't look at her. She was too focused on Jack. He was her responsibility until he entered that gate. She wouldn't let a flirting Allie sidetrack her.

Allie put her hand on Harley's shoulder and rested on it, putting her lips almost next to Harley's ear. Harley tried to shoo her away, her hand coming dangerously close to Allie's face as she blew into Harley's ear. "Harley…"

Harley sniffed, and then she was sprinting across the playground. Pulling her gun from her waistband, she lifted it and pointed in Jack's direction.

"Duck, Jack."

"What?"

"Get the fuck down."

Jack fell across his mother, taking her to the ground. A Dark Soul materialized where Jack had been standing. Putting the barrel against his head, Harley pulled the trigger. Acid black fog replaced his dark form.

"Get up," Harley commanded. Reaching down, she pulled Jack to a standing position, his mother getting up at the same time. "Run for the gate."

"What about my mom?"

"Run, both of you," she yelled as another Dark Soul pushed through the fog.

The contrast of the fog and the Dark Soul was eerie. The Dark Soul's body seemed to eat the fog, wisps of it trailing him as he chased Jack and his mother.

Jack's mom wouldn't be able to go through the gate unless Harley did something, something unexpected.

Harley pushed her body, her legs barely able to catch him before he tried to kill Jack. The soul raised his arm, a blade cutting through the air, just missing Jack's mother. They weren't after Jack, at least not this Dark Soul. They were chasing Jack's mom.

"Stop," Harley screamed.

The Dark Soul hesitated just long enough to give Harley the extra seconds she needed to close in on him. She jumped on him and pinned him to the ground, reaching into his chest. He would be able to see her and she wanted him to; she wanted him to face death.

"You're going to die, Paladin," he growled.

"Not tonight." She squeezed his heart tighter.

"Don't be so sure. My gatekeeper is here and—"

Harley felt his last beat in her hand as she squeezed his heart to extinction. She closed her eyes and reveled in the feeling of revenge she'd just exacted. Her body shook with a surge of power. Clenching her fists tighter, she tried to control the convulsion. She stood gasping for air, her lungs on fire. She couldn't see peripherally. She seemed to be looking through a tube.

"Harley?" Dawn touched Harley's shoulder. Calm enveloped her immediately and she regained her normal sight.

"Jack?"

"Right here," he said, holding up his hand, his other hand clasping his mother's.

"You need to get through that gate, Jack."

"I'm not leaving her. I can't." He kissed the back of his mother's hand.

The sentimental moment fractured when two

more Dark Souls pounced through the dense fog. Each one ran full speed at Jack and his mother. Harley raised her hands, palms facing the souls. Without thinking she pushed at them, sending them reeling backward. Allie pointed her hand at them, exploding them in an instant.

"Jack, you need to cross. Now," Harley yelled.

She needed a reprieve from the onslaught of souls attacking them. She could barely wrap her mind around what she'd just done—sending the souls backward without touching them. How could she do that? Protectors had those kinds of powers.

"This is your fault, Alleo. You need to fix your mistake. Send his mother with him."

Crossing her arms, Allie let out a spurt of air, signaling her disgust with Dawn's idea. "I had nothing to do with the death of her Paladin. That is all Lucius's fault."

"Are you a Protector or a gatekeeper?" Harley asked.

"I haven't decided."

Harley was getting irritated as she watched Allie pick at something under her nails.

"You get a choice?"

"Oh, you have so much to learn, Paladin," she said and then smirked at Harley. "I'll be happy to teach you everything you need to know about being a Paladin and then some."

Harley could sense danger coming. Jack was so close to his gate all he had to do was turn and take a step. His death grip on his mother's hand was going to present a problem though. So without giving it a second thought, she walked up to Jack and whispered into his ear.

"Don't let go of your mother's hand."

"Huh?"

"Hold tight," she said

Stepping back a few steps, Harley hunched down and ran into him like a nose tackle. Jack fell backward into his gate, pulling his mother with him.

"What have you done?" Allie said, stepping toward the closing gate. She slipped her hand in and swished it around, pulling it out before the portal was completely sealed.

Harley looked back at Dawn, who winked at Harley and gave her a half-smile.

Clap.

Clap.

Clap.

"Well done, Paladin. Well played," Lucius said, walking toward them. An army of Dark Souls vibrated behind him. The crowd surged and receded, clearly gearing up for an attack. They were just waiting for the signal from Lucius.

Dawn stepped from the group and in front of her brother. "What are you doing here, Lucius?"

Harley wished she hadn't done that. She stood in Harley's direct path to Lucius.

"Well, dear Sister, of course I'm here to speak to the Paladin."

"We don't have anything to talk about, Lucius." Harley stepped up and stood next to Dawn, gripping the gun in her right hand tighter. She didn't want Lucius figuring out what she had planned, so she cleared her mind and focused on Jack and his mother's journey. She hoped he picked wisely when he was presented with his next life. Perhaps he and his mother would journey together. She could only wonder what happened on the other side, since her journey was cemented, and choice didn't seem to be an option for her.

"That was a fantastic finishing move. Did you know she was going to do that, Allie?" He focused on his sister. If Harley hadn't known better, she would think he was fuming at the woman who only last night he was trying to tempt Harley with.

"Really now, Brother. This isn't your business." Allie stood defiant. It was clear to Harley she wasn't about to let her brother bully her. But why had she let him kill her Paladin? These relationships baffled her at every level. Was Allie a Protector or a gatekeeper? Did she play both sides when it suited her? The only things she was sure of was that Dawn was one of the good guys, Lucius was the devil incarnate—she had the memories to prove it—and Allie couldn't be trusted.

"Well, it is my business, Allie dear. We have a deal. Or don't you remember?" He walked into her space and in a split second had lifted her off the ground by the throat. He sneered. "You broke the deal and—"

Harley snapped into action. Raising her hand, she pushed her palm toward Lucius and knocked him off balance, so that he dropped Allie. Within the blink of an eye, she hoisted up her 9mm, pointed it at his chest, and pulled the trigger.

"No."

Pop.

Pop.

Something broadsided Harley and everything went black.

Chapter Thirty

W̱ake up, Harley. Please, please wake up." Harley couldn't see around her, but the voice was familiar. Renee. Something pushed her forward, toward the light. She didn't want to move. She wanted to stay rooted to where she was, because going ahead would mean she'd lose Dawn. She just knew it. Another shove and she was fully engulfed in the light.

"Harley. Oh, my God, Harley. Your eyes are open." Renee threw herself across Harley's body, practically crushing her.

"Off," Harley whispered.

"What?"

"Get off me." Harley's voice sounded more like something being moved across sandpaper. "Water."

A straw was quickly placed in her mouth. She pulled hard, but it was being pinched off.

"Not too much. You've been out for weeks. I don't want you to choke," Renee said, easing up on the pressure so a trickle of water coated the back of her mouth.

Barely opening her eyes, she turned her head away from the bright light of the window. As she shaded her gaze she spotted Renee and, right behind her, Dawn. Her blue aura vibrated like it always did when she looked at Harley. Harley couldn't mistake the loving look from Dawn. Without thinking, she smiled.

"Oh, Harley, I was so worried." Renee filled her

view of the world she'd just reentered.

Harley turned her head and caught the flash of a dark shadow moving past her room door. Startled, she turned back toward Dawn.

"Harley, what's wrong? You look like you've seen a ghost."

"Up," Harley commanded. "Sit me up."

As Renee pressed a button, the bed put Harley into a seated position. The monitors she was connected to went off as her heart rate accelerated, the pressure in her head making it feel like it was going to explode.

"Get out."

"What?"

"Out." Harley pointed to the door. "Go find that bitch you cheated on me with and get out of my life."

"Harley you don't know what you're saying. You're confused. You've had a traumatic brain injury. You're...you're confused." Renee pulled on Harley's hand and kissed the back of it. "I love you, Harley."

Harley looked at Dawn, still standing behind Renee, and then back to Renee. "I don't love you. Leave now."

When Renee didn't move Harley started yelling. "Nurse, nurse. Where's that damn button? Fuck, my head."

Harley's head was splitting. The bright lights of the room kept her from opening her eyes.

"Where's my mom. Mom? Mom?"

A woman ran into the room and to the side off the bed. "Oh, dear Jesus, Harley. I'm right here, honey."

Harley coughed as she tried to talk.

"Renee, don't just sit there. Get the doctor." Her mother had missed the whole commotion, but it didn't matter. Renee was as good as gone. There was no way

Harley was letting that bitch back into her room, let alone her life.

"Right." Renee's voice sounded quick and raspy. "Oh, God, Harley. I'm so glad you're alive."

Renee kissed her hand and then planted one on Harley's forehead. Cupping Harley's face, she forced Harley to look at her. "I love you, baby. You had us so worried." Renee raced out of the room yelling for the doctor and nurses.

Harley looked from Dawn to her mother and then back again. Couldn't her mother see Dawn? She was right there. Dawn shook her head and stepped forward, grabbing her hand.

She can't see me, Harley. Only you can do that. Remember?

No, I guess I didn't.

It's okay. I'm here. I'll never be far away.

I love you, Harley said, staring at Dawn.

I love you, too, but then you've always known that, haven't you?

I think so. I just never wanted to believe it. I knew it would make me stay, be a Paladin.

That's a decision only you can make. You can't avoid your destiny. It will find you.

Dawn smiled, kissed Harley's hand, and disappeared.

"Don't go."

"I'm not going anywhere, honey."

Harley hesitated, waiting for Dawn to come back. When she didn't, she turned to her mom and whispered, "Thanks, Mom."

"I love you, honey."

"I love you too, Mom."

"Why would you try to hurt yourself, honey?"

Swallowing hard, Harley shook her head. "I didn't, Mom."

"What?"

"I didn't shoot myself. I'm right-handed."

"What, honey? You're not making any sense."

She lifted her hand, made a gun symbol, and pointed to the right side of her head.

"Oh, my God, I never even thought of that. I was just so worried about you. Saving you was all I could think about."

"It's okay."

God, it had all been a dream. She was still in her hospital bed with a hole in her head, tubes and lines flowing out of her body to a machine that kept her alive. Dark Souls, talk of Paladins and gatekeepers were all just the dreams of a medication-induced psychosis.

"Thank God," Harley whispered.

"What, honey?" Her mom moved closer, kissing Harley's hand.

She had just enough energy to shake her head, whispering, "Nothing."

She wouldn't weigh her mother down with her wild rantings. It was bad enough she thought she was crazy. Add a head injury, and she was surely bound for the psych ward.

"Well, Harley, you sure gave us a scare. How are you feeling?"

Her eyelid was lifted and a light forced into her eye. Then the other had the same treatment. She cleared her throat, ready to answer. Looking up, she saw the doctor from her dreams standing beside her. Only he wasn't alone. A dark energy surrounded him as he moved around the bed and looked at her chart.

Harley flinched as he reached for her head. "Don't touch me."

"Harley, he's been taking care of you all of this time. Calm down, honey. I know you've probably got a lot of questions, but let him check you out first."

"No. I don't want him touching me."

"Harley, I'm sure this is just the effects of your head trauma. I'm Doctor Wells. I'm sure all of this is confusing, but..." Suddenly he slowed down his speech, as if it would help her understand. "You've. had. a. serious. head. injury. You. might. be. in. some. pain—"

Harley held up her hand. "Stop. I understand you perfectly. I want another doctor, now."

"But—" He touched her arm, transferring energy into her body.

"Argh, you're hurting me. Get the fuck away from me, now," she screamed.

"I'll get a sedative." The doctor looked at Harley's mom and then left them alone. Harley didn't like him, she didn't trust him, and she'd be damned if she was going to let him give her anything.

Renee touched her other arm. "Harley, calm down, honey."

"Get her out of here, Mom. I don't want her anywhere around me. Go find your girlfriend, you cheating bitch."

Everyone in the room stopped and looked at Renee.

"Sweetheart, I don't know what you're talking about. You've had a bad accident and are having some delusional thoughts." A blush ran up Renee's neck and colored her face.

Oh, Harley was having delusions all right. She was dreaming of putting her hands around Renee's neck and choking the life out of her.

"Get out, now." Harley turned to her mom. "Get her out of here now, please."

"Of course. Come on, Renee. She's getting too worked up. I think if it's best if you leave." Harley's mom escorted her to the door and whispered, "I'll call you in the morning."

"Dim the lights, Mom. They're hurting my head." Harley reached up and felt the bandage. She knew that a hole lay under the protective covering. The room darkened and Harley relaxed.

"I need to speak to you, Mom," she said, reaching for her mother.

"Save your strength, honey. We've got plenty of time to talk."

Both of them jumped as something hit the window.

"What the heck was that?" her mom said.

"A bird. There'll be more. That's what I need to tell you."

"What? How do you know it's a bird?"

"I just do."

"Honey, you need to try to relax."

"Mom, whatever you do, don't let that doctor touch me, please. If you love me, you won't let him touch me."

"Calm down, honey. I'll take care of you. Don't worry."

"Thanks, Mom." Harley closed her eyes and relaxed back into the pillow.

The door opened and Harley could hear her mom talking to the doctor. She was in good hands, but something was happening. Peering through barely raised lids, she caught sight of the doctor putting something in her IV, her mom standing next to him.

"Relax, honey. It's just something to calm you down." She patted Harley's hand reassuringly.

"Aw, Mom…"

Chapter Thirty-one

Harley shifted in her bed, the noise of the hospital outside her door waking her. Punching the button on her bed, she raised the head of her bed so she could sit up. Her bladder screamed at her to take care of business. Without lighting, it was almost impossible to find the call button. Screw it. Nature was calling and wasn't going to wait for the nurse. Pulling her blankets off, she swung her legs over the edge and sat waiting. Her head spun. As she looked down, it suddenly seemed like a long drop to the floor. Whatever the doctor had given her was working overtime on her body.

Maybe she should wait.

A noise in the corner pulled at her attention.

"Mom?"

Peering into the darkness she saw a lone figure sitting in the shadow of the corner of her room.

"Mom?"

It didn't move. It didn't respond. It only sat there.

"Who are you?"

The figure stood and walked toward her. "Hello, Harley."

Dawn.

"Christ, it wasn't a dream, was it?" Harley had thought she'd imagined Dawn in her room earlier. At least she wasn't losing her marbles, yet. The rest of what had happened earlier was debatable.

Dawn stood before Harley. Their bodies touched. Harley could barely hold her head up as she tried to look at Dawn.

"How are you feeling?" Dawn ran her fingers through the tangled locks and then lifted Harley's chin to look at her.

"Like I've been pulled ass first through a hole the size of a—" Stopping, she stared at Dawn's lips and suddenly had the urge to kiss them.

The last few days raced back and hit her square. "What are you doing here, Dawn?"

Dawn smiled and gently placed a kiss on Harley's lips before she answered. "I'm your Protector. Don't you remember?"

"I'm not sure if I remember what's real and what's a dream."

"It wasn't a dream, Harley. It was all real. You got Jack to his gate, and even better, you got his mom through too."

"I can't believe any of that was real. Honestly, I think it's all a result of all the pain medication they gave me." Harley grabbed the rail of the bed and wiggled closer to the edge. Putting up her hand she said, "When I wake up it will all be the same as it was before. You're just a result of my overactive imagination. You're not real." Harley wrestled with her mind and closed her eyes, hoping that when she opened them no one would be in the room, especially her mom. If she was sitting in that chair, she had just witnessed her daughter losing her mind.

"Harley," Dawn whispered. Raising her hand, she opened her palm, causing Harley's birthmark to itch.

Harley pulled her gown down and noticed the addition of the moon line and another line under what was now a blue tattoo.

"What the hell is that?"

"You added another Paladin line when you saved Jack's mother." Dawn traced it with her fingertip. "Now do you believe me?"

"That means I have to believe in evil like Lucius. I'm not sure I'm ready to take that leap."

Harley grabbed the hand. It was warm, flesh, and attached to a woman she knew she was in love with. That was real. Kissing the palm, she pulled it to her face and placed it against her cheek. Dawn's energy wrapped around her—freeing, calming, and inviting. Could she turn her back on what they'd shared and return to her normal life? How could she deny Dawn?

Lucius.

The last thing she remembered was aiming her gun at the gatekeeper, firing, and then being knocked sideways. Did waking up in the hospital mean she was done being a Paladin? She had so many questions.

"Is Lucius dead?"

"I don't know."

"What do you mean, you don't know? You were standing there when I shot him."

"I saw you with the gun. I worried that if you missed he'd kill you instantly, so I morphed you back here to protect you. By the time I turned around, he was gone."

"No shit." Harley leaned against the back of the bed. "I can't catch a break, can I?"

"I think you being alive is catching a break."

"Allie?"

"Mother is looking for her. I suspect she'll have a lot of explaining to do about the death of her Paladin when Mother finds her."

"I don't understand."

"A Protector is supposed to give their life for their Paladin. She didn't protect hers, so Mother will want some answers."

"What happens now?" Harley motioned to Dawn and then herself. "With us. I'm here and in this body. Doesn't that limit what we can do?"

A thump hit the outside. Another kamikaze bird.

Thump.

Thump.

"I guess that answers my questions."

Dawn threaded her fingers through Harley's, pulled them to her lips, and kissed them.

"I can put the word out that you've died. It will give you time to get a new life, in a new city and off the radar for a while. It isn't much, but it means we can never see each other again. Or..."

The silence lingered between them, of them looking at the other, searching for an answer.

"Or, I can accept who I am."

"There's that." Dawn offered a half-smile. "I can stick around and we can work through all of this, answer those questions you have, and get souls to their gate."

Harley nodded. "You know I'm still going to kill Lucius and the other gatekeepers."

"I know."

"Are you okay with that?"

Dawn shrugged. "I won't help you kill them, Harley. I can't."

"I know, but I can't let Lucius get away with killing my mother. I mean my mother in the past. Obviously he didn't kill my real mother. I mean my current mother." She was babbling and confident she wasn't making any sense. "I mean—"

"I know what you mean, Harley." Dawn stroked Harley's face. "Why don't you go to sleep, and we can talk about all of this stuff later."

"I gotta pee," Harley reminded Dawn.

"I can fix that," Dawn said, swishing her hand around Harley's body.

"Wow. I'll remember that next time we're in a tight spot."

Dawn winked at her and then flashed her an irresistible grin.

Harley pulled Dawn close, reaching up for a kiss. Their energy mingled as Harley deepened the kiss and let her hands roam over Dawn's body. Leaning back, she pulled Dawn on top of her. Suddenly she felt better.

"Are you working your magic?"

"Maybe," Dawn said, nipping at Harley's chin. "Is it working?"

"Maybe."

"Well, if it's questionable, perhaps I need to try harder."

"Give it a shot," Harley said.

Dawn's wings unfurled as Harley's hand traveled down her back and pushed herself against Dawn's hips. Deepening the kiss even more, Harley slipped her tongue against Dawn's lips, begging for entrance.

"You know we're in a hospital bed, right?"

"So."

"Someone could walk in and see you writhing in pleasure. How would you explain that?"

"I'm sure they already think I'm nuts when I kicked out that doctor we saw in the hospital before."

"The one with the dark soul?" Dawn tensed.

"Don't go there. Let's have one moment together

before all hell breaks loose again." Harley kissed Dawn's neck, slipping down to her chest. "Besides, I think I'll be gone before he gets back tomorrow."

"Feeling that good, are you?"

"You could say that." Harley ventured lower.

"Well, don't let me stop your recovery."

"You aren't, but you could help by taking off those clothes."

"Hmm."

ᴧ.ᴧᴎᴕᴕ

A chill filled the hospital as Lucius walked the hallways. He knew his next victim was here somewhere. It was only a matter of time before he found her and settled the score. He stopped, pulled a cigar, clipped the end, and lit it. Taking a long pull, he held it, savoring the smoke, and then barely opening his mouth, he let the smoke ease its way out.

"Damn, that's good. Now where is that bitch?"

About the author

Award winning, international best selling author, Isabella, lives in California with her wife and three sons. Isabella's first novel, Always Faithful, won a GCLS award in the Traditional Contemporary Romance category in 2010. She was also a finalist in the International Book Awards, and an Honorable Mention in the 2010 and 2012 Rainbow Awards.

She is a member of the Rainbow Romance Writers, Romance Writers of America and the Gold Crown Literary Society. She has written several short stories and working on her next novel, Cigar Barons - A family dynasty where blood isn't thicker than water, it's war!

You can follow Isabella on Facebook, Twitter and Instagram

Facebook - www.facebook.com/isabella
Twiter - www.twitter.com/@Isabella_SBP
Instagram - Isabella_Author

Other books by Isabella

Award winning novel - Always Faithful
ISBN - 978-0-9828608-0-9

Major Nichol "Nic" Caldwell is the only survivor of her helicopter crash in Iraq. She is left alone to wonder why she and she alone. Survivor's guilt has nothing on the young Major as she is forced to deal with the scars, both physical and mental, left from her ordeal overseas. Before the accident, she couldn't think of doing anything else in her life.

Claire Monroe is your average military wife, with a loving husband and a little girl. She is used to the time apart from her husband. In fact, it was one of the reasons she married him. Then, one day, her life is turned upside down when she gets a visit from the Marine Corps.

Can these two women come to terms with the past and finally find happiness, or will their shared sense of honor keep them apart?

Forever Faithful
ISBN - 978-1-939062-75-8

Life is what happens when you make other plans, and Nic and Claire have just found out that life and the Marine Corps have other plans for their lives.

Nic Caldwell has served her country, met the woman of her dreams, and has reached the rank of Lieutenant

Colonel. She's studying at one of the nation's most prestigious military universities, setting her sights on a research position after graduation. Things couldn't be better and then it happens; a sudden assignment to Afghanistan derails any thoughts of marriage and wedded bliss. Another combat zone, another tragedy, and Nic suddenly finds herself fighting for her life.

Claire Monroe loves her new life in Monterey. She's finally where she wants to be, getting ready to start her master's program at the local university, watching her daughter, Grace, growing up, and getting ready to marry the love of her life. What could possibly derail a perfect life? The Marine Corps.

Will Nic survive Afghanistan? Can Claire step up and be the strength in their relationship? Or will this overseas assignment and a catastrophic accident divide their once happy home?

Broken Shield
ISBN - 978-0-9828608-2-3

Tyler Jackson, former paramedic now firefighter, has seen her share of death up close. The death of her wife caused Tyler to rethink her career choices, but the death of her mother two weeks later cemented her return to the ranks of firefighter. Her path of self-destruction and womanizing is just a front to hide the heartbreak and devastation she lives with every day. Tyler's given up on finding love and having the family she's always wanted. When tragedy strikes her life for a second time she finds something she thought she lost.

Ashley Henderson loves her job. Ignoring her mother's advice, she opts for a career in law enforcement. But, Ashley hides a secret that soon turns her life upside down. Shame, guilt and fear keep Ashley from venturing forward and finding the love she so desperately craves. Her life comes crashing down around her in one swift moment forcing her to come clean about her secrets and her life.

Can two women thrust together by one traumatic event survive and find love together, or will their past force them apart?

American Yakuza
ISBN - 978-0-9828608-3-0

Luce Potter straddles three cultures as she strives to live with the ideals of family, honor, and duty. When her grandfather passes the family business to her, Luce finds out that power, responsibility and justice come with a price. Is it a price she's willing to die for?
Brooke Erickson lives the fast-paced life of an investigative journalist living on the edge until it all comes crashing down around her one night in Europe. Stateside, Brooke learns to deal with a new reality when she goes to work at a financial magazine and finds out things aren't always as they seem.

Can two women find enough common ground for love or will their two different worlds and cultures keep them apart?

Executive Disclosure
ISBN - 978-0-9828608-3-0

When a life is threatened, it takes a special breed of person to step in front of a bullet. Chad Morgan's job has put her life on the line more times that she can count. Getting close to the client is expected; getting too close could be deadly for Chad. Reagan Reynolds wants the top job at Reynolds Holdings and knows how to play the game like "the boys". She's not above using her beauty and body as currency to get what she wants. Shocked to find out someone wants her dead, Reagan isn't thrilled at the prospect of needing protection as she tries to convince the board she's the right woman for a man's job. How far will a killer go to get what they want? Secrets and deception twist the rules of the game as a killer closes in. How far will Chad go to protect her beautiful, but challenging client?

American Yakuza II - The Lies that Bind
ISBN - 978-10939062-20-8

Luce Potter runs her life and her business with an iron fist and complete control until lies and deception unravel her world. The shadow of betrayal consumes Luce, threatening to destroy the most precious thing in her life, Brooke Erickson.

Brooke Erickson finds herself on the outside of Luce's life looking in. As events spiral out of control Brooke can only watch as the woman she loves pushes her further away. Suddenly, devastated and alone, Brooke refuses to let go without an explanation.

Colby Water, a federal agent investigating the ever-elusive Luce Potter, discovers someone from her past is front and center in her investigation of the Yakuza crime leader. Before she can put the crime boss in prison, she must confront the ultimate deception in her professional life.

When worlds collide, betrayal, dishonor and death are inevitable. Can Luce and Brooke survive the explosion?

Razor's Edge
ISBN: 978-1-943353-81-1

Luce Potter lives by a code of honor. Push her and she shoves back, harder. There's only one problem: Luce has just found out that revenge is a knife that cuts both ways. Now that her lover Brooke has survived the attack on her life, Luce has only one thing on her mind, and his name is Frank. Unfortunately, someone walks into her life that she didn't see coming.

Brooke Erickson has survived an attack so brutal it's left a permanent scar on her soul. All she wants to do now is go home and finish recuperating with her lover, Luce Potter, by her side. An unexpected event puts Brooke at the head of the Yakuza family. Can she command the respect necessary to lead it through the crisis?

Luce and Brooke's worlds are upending. Can each do what's necessary to survive and return to a new normal?

Surviving Reagan
ISBN - 978-1-939062-38-3

Chad Morgan has finally worked through the betrayal of her former client and lover, Reagan Reynolds. Putting the pieces of her life back in order, she finds herself on a collision course with that past when she takes on a new client, the future first lady. Unfortunately, Chad's newest job puts her in the cross-hairs of a domestic terrorist determined to release a virus that could kill thousands of women.

Reagan Reynolds has paid for her sins and is ready to start a new life. Attending a business conference in Abu Dhabi gives her the opportunity to prove to her father and herself that she's worthy of a fresh start. Her past will intersect with her future at the conference when she accidentally comes face-to-face with Chad Morgan.

Time is running out. Will Reagan confront Chad? Can she convince Chad she's changed, or will death part them forever?

Writing as Jett Abbott

Scarlet Masquerade
ISBN - 978-0-982860-81-6

What do you say to the woman you thought died over a century ago? Will time heal all wounds or does it just allow them to fester and grow? A.J. Locke has lived over two centuries and works like a demon, both figuratively and literally. As the owner of a successful pharmaceutical company that specializes in blood research, she has changed the way she can live her life. Wanting for nothing, she has smartly compartmentalized her life so that when she needs to, she can pick up and start all over again, which happens every twenty years or so. Love is not an emotion A.J.

spends much time on. Since losing the love of her life to the plague one hundred fifty years ago, she vowed to never travel down that road again. That isn't to say she doesn't have women when she wants them, she just wants them on her terms and that doesn't involve a long term commitment.

A.J.'s cool veneer is peeled back when she sees the love of her life in a lesbian bar, in the same town, in the same day and time in which she lives. Is her mind playing tricks on her? If not, how did Clarissa survive the plague when she had made A.J. promise never to change her?

Clarissa Graham is a university professor who has lived an obscure life teaching English literature. She has made it a point to stay off the radar and never become involved with anything that resembles her past life. Every once in a while Clarissa has an itch that needs to be scratched, so she finds an out of the way location to scratch it. She keeps her personal life separate from her professional one, and in doing so she is able to keep her secrets to herself. Suddenly, her life is turned upside down when someone tries to kill her. She finds herself in the middle of an assassination plot with no idea who wants her dead

Scarlet Assassin
ISBN 978-1-939062-36-9

Selene Hightower is a killer for hire. A vampire who walks in both the light and the darkness, but lately darkness has a stronger pull. Her unfinished business could cost her the ability to live in the light, throwing her permanently back into the black ink of evil.

Doctor Francesca Swartz led a boring life filled with test tubes, blood trials, and work. One exploratory night, in a world of leather and torture, she is intrigued by a dark and solitary soul. She surrenders to temptation and the desire to experience something new, only to discover that it might alter her life forever.

Will Selene allow the light to win over the darkness threatening the edges of her life? Two women wonder if they can co-exist despite vast differences, as worlds collide and threaten to destroy any hope of happiness. Who will win?

CPSIA information can be obtained
at www.ICGtesting.com
Printed in the USA
LVOW12s2101091117
555655LV00003B/321/P